The

Last Return

A novel

by

Axelan Ziba

This book is a work of fiction. Names, characters, places
and incidents are either products of the author's
imagination or are used fictitiously. Any resemblance to
actual events or locales or persons, living or dead, is
entirely coincidental.

LIBRARY AND ARCHIVES CANADA CATALOGUING IN
PUBLICATION
Ziba, Axelan. Author
The Last Return /Axelan Ziba
ISBN 978-0-9958262-1-2 (softcover)

Editor: Chris Banner

Printed in Canada

Produced by Ziba Press, Victoria. BC. Canada.

Dedication

This book is dedicated to my wife. She introduced me to the reality dimension of existence. She taught me how to realize my inner-self and to discover the unlimited ability and desire within. Living and working in a busy city had entirely occupied my life and never left any space left for recognizing such phenomenal knowledge. Meeting my wife, with her calm and assuring character compelled me to gain knowledge of her practice. With her help and direction I entered a new gate of life where I could see right within. To my wife, I am always grateful for her kind heart and feel blessed to share my life on earth with her.

I am Theo, a soul who has celebrated thousands of birthdays. In my first human incarnations I was an immature soul struggling to understand spiritual wisdom. Initially my soul was as transparent as an aura, but as my wisdom grew, my soul took on color until I became a shining example to fledgling spirits of my world.

Chapter 1.
Inspiration as a spirit

"Soldiers, soldiers have come. They're at the farm. They've got Mummy and our sisters and have set the house on fire." Juliet, my youngest sister, screamed, running across the field.

Leo, my father picked her up and hugged her.

"It'll be alright. Go with your brother Lance. I'll go back and see what's causing the fuss." My father looked at me. "Take your sister and hide in the woods. Don't come to the house. I'll come and get you. Go quickly."

He turned, picked up his scythe and ran across the field.

He looked full of life, but that was the last time I saw him alive. I took my sister's hand and hurried into the forest. I knew an old hollow tree that was a great hiding place. I suspected it was a bear's den in the winter, but in mid-summer it was empty.

Inside, the tree was damp and dark apart from the sliver of shaded light that glimmered through the entrance.

"It smells in here."

"Be quiet. It's safe." I muttered to Juliet. We crouched together in the deepest part of the hollow. I put my arm protectively around her and waited and waited.

"I must go and see what is happening." I said to Juliet.

"Don't leave me," she said. "I'm scared."

"It won't be for long and you're safe here." I replied.

"But father said not to go to the house."

"I know, but it has been awhile. I'm sure the soldiers have gone. I'll be back before you know it." I slipped out of the tree and ran quietly through the forest. At sixteen years old, I was the son, and almost a man. I emerged from the forest, seeing smoke spiraling into the sky from their clearing. Throwing aside caution, I ran full speed toward their farm.

Flames roared in the thatch roof and my sisters, tied to the porch, wailed and screamed, pulling at their bindings. I did not see any soldiers. I undid my sister's ropes, carrying them to safety before searching the smoke-filled house. My eyes burned in the heat and I coughed, breathing in smoke. I held a rag to my mouth but could barely breathe by the time I discovered my mother's blood soaked body, laying abandoned on the floor. This was no time for emotion, I grabbed her lifeless body and lifted, trying to carry her. I couldn't see a foot before me and tears ran down my cheeks as I struggled to carry her out the backdoor. Rushing out, I saw my father's body, killed by a long sword still embedded in his back. My father had died trying to save his wife.

I left the lifeless, tortured body of my mother by Leo's and ran toward my two sisters. On the way I grabbed a bucket of water and poured it over them. They sat up shocked and scared. I hugged them, "Go hide in the stable in case the soldiers return." I urged. I held my mother's inert body, shook her, screamed at her and begged her half burned body not to die. The soldiers had beaten her and left her to die. I looked at my father's lifeless body, while kneeling and crying to my mother.

Confused and full of emotion I screamed for help but no one came. I covered their bodies and removed the sword from my father's back. Tears streamed down my face and my hands ran with their blood, raising the sword, I vowed vengeance to my wounded heart. "I will carry my father's message to all the farmers."

I gathered a few tools and vital possessions before taking my sisters to my uncle, Toran, and making sure they were safe. Their livestock, a cow, two goats and three pigs had gone with the soldiers in a wagon. I did not find their geese or chickens and suspected the soldiers had taken them too.

Toran, a widower, took us in, looking after us like his own. He was a farmer, struggling to provide for his family and welcomed my help on the farm. The fields he worked were poor and flinty and never yielded good crops, although the king still demanded heavy taxes. Toran's few scrawny chickens scuffled in the dirt looking for plump bugs, but only found meager fare.

Toran worked hard but lost his youngest child to pneumonia and it devastated him as though he'd lost all joy in life. But he constantly exhorted other farmers not to pay the king's heavy taxes but sadly died at the age of fifty-four, malnourished and in poverty.

As I matured, so did my courage. I led farmers against the king's troops and stole back the taxes. My father's followers, respecting my courage, helped me. Having learned weapons themselves, they taught me the bow, the sword, the pike and more. I absorbed their teachings like a sponge, but they also counselled me to use my intelligence to encourage the soldiers to turn against the king. My words and humanitarian heart became my greatest weapons, in mesmerizing and transfixing them. I showed them how to understand their freedom by joining with the people to stop the king's cruelty. Some soldiers hearing of my audacity, sought to challenge me but encountering my purity, they abandoned thoughts of fighting against me.

After years of quarrel and skirmishes, my reputation as a fearless warrior who followed my heart fighting against injustice, spread and grew.

One night, I intervened to save a man from harassment, but the soldiers captured and imprisoned me. The king, aware of my reputation and my love of people, wanted me to kneel before him and be humiliated. Yet despite torture and deprivation, I refused to kneel even though the king promised to alleviate my suffering if I complied.

The king, fearing people's reaction, kept me in jail, torturing and trying to force me to declare my obedience. But I didn't kneel or surrender. Finally, following the king's orders, guards burned-out my eyes and took me into the forest to execute me.

In darkness, the soldiers carried me into the forest, leaving me and my assassin by the cold river, although I remained conscious, I still urged the soldiers to be kind to farmers and villagers.

One assassin remained behind to kill me. That young soldier, affected by my teaching, lied to the others. "I have killed him and buried him beneath the bushes. The wild boar will eat his body." I, Theo, inhabited the spirit of that soldier. I was called Dion.

—o0o—

My duty was to kill Lance, but looking into his kind face, recognizing his spirit and hearing his uplifting words, I was spellbound and did not kill him. Instead I hid him in the bushes, leaving him water to survive.

I chose to be Dion because my challenge was to discover my courage and therefore advance my soul. I reported to my captain about killing Lance but I lied and pretended I'd killed him, showing him my bloody hands but knew if my lies were discovered, I would hang.

For some reason, after witnessing Lance's bravery, I found his purity overpowering and irresistible. I had to protect this beloved hero from further harm.

I returned to the forest as soon as possible to help him. Questioning, "What have I done?" I kept asking myself, checking to make sure no one followed. I walked quickly but cautiously, although I jumped whenever a twig cracked beneath my feet. Moonlight slipped between the thick layers of darkness and danced on the tree branches while dense clouds hung in the sky pressing down on me. Silence was the only sound except when I snapped a branch beneath my feet. Thoughts of being caught flooded my paranoid mind and I feared every shadow. Pushing away branches as I crept through the undergrowth, I questioned, why I had helped the king's enemy? "What ifs" crowded my mind, but whenever I thought of Lance, I knew I was right to save him and crept on even faster.

Lance's courage and gentleness stayed in my thoughts, as did memories of his torture which had thankfully not weakened him. He was unafraid, continuing to broadcast his message, urging soldiers to protect the villagers against the villainous king who ruled them. He clarified my thoughts, encouraging me to protect him. My small soldier's wage was not worth killing such an outstanding man. My actions had been right so I promised to help. I had left him close to the river and by drinking water, had gained strength and his blindness ensured he would not wander.

"Praise God, you are alive."

"Yes," he grinned. "I filled the skin with water from the river. I nearly fell in the first time, but I am growing aware of my other senses. My hearing and my touch tell me almost as much as my eyes. I heard you creeping in the trees, so I knew someone was coming. I am so glad it is you."

I was pleased to see him and was sure we were becoming friends.

That night, I carried Lance deeper into the bush, building a hideaway inside a hollow tree but still close to the river. I cleaned his wounds, fed him from food I had brought, let him rest and regain his strength.

I remained by his side for days and became his eyes and eventually became his partner by returning tax money to the people stolen back from their cruel king.

I had been a good soldier, but Lance taught me to be a brigand and outlaw. He opened my mind, "Why should the lord grow fat as we grow thin?" He asked. He taught me to use my anger and vengeance as weapons of peace. "Think," he said, "Every king's soldier is a potential ally. We just have to show them what is right."

I was honored to be his companion and, although sightless, he used all senses and clearly understood our problems. Our following grew as we successfully helped farmers rob the king's tax collectors. We encouraged farmers in surrounding villages to stand up for their rights. We become the most wanted outlaws in the land and the king placed a heavy price on our heads.

We crouched in the forest, next to the trail to the king's castle.

"They are coming, I hear them," Lance whispered. I waved my arm signaling to the others. Then, hearing the tramp of feet and the grinding of heavy wagon wheels in the dry dirt of the trail, I signaled again.

"The wagon is laden," Lance muttered. "This should be a good haul." He smiled into the forest, but I knew he was smiling at me.

Staring across the forested green gloom, I saw the sparkle of the soldiers' mail and the glint of their weapons. The officer was mounted on a heavy stallion, while the company of troops trudged behind. Beyond them was the creaking, grinding wagon, pulled by four horses. 'Yes, this will be a good haul,' I thought.

I signaled again, and a tree crashed across the trail in front of the officer. His horse reared, almost unseating him, before he drew his sword, unhitched his shield and turned back to face his men. Before he shouted an order, two arrows thumped into his chest and he gurgled and coughed, falling from his horse. The horse galloped into the forest, crashing through the shrubs and thickets like a demented mustang. The foot soldiers, the few standing after another flight of arrows thinned their number, fled to the wagon, forming a tight circle around and beneath it.

"More horses," I hear them, muttered Lance. "We must retreat. We are too few."

I waved my sword above my head and screamed, "Retreat, soldiers are coming." Mounted soldiers thundered into the clearing, closely followed by another troop, running on foot. They cut down our fleeing bowmen and as I led Lance away from the fray, a mounted horseman bounded up behind us.

"Yield!" he screamed as his horse blocked our escape.

I laid down my sword and shield and took Lance's arm.

"It is over," I muttered.

We were tied to the back of the wagon and walked to the castle.

The king immediately pronounced our sentence.

"Death, by beheading. At daylight tomorrow."

A crowd gathered in the courtyard of the castle as we were led to the block.

Lance went first and the crowd booed as his head rolled into the waiting basket. I slowly removed my leather helm, handed it to the guard, knelt before the bloody block and bent my head. My world went black as the sword severed my head.

The guards placed our heads on the city gate on pikes as a lesson, hoping to terrify the people, but our actions became a legend among the people, encouraging them to resist the king's draconian taxes.

I always hold dear the memory of my life as Dion, not only because of the courageous bravery I learned but I also found out that Lance was in reality my spirit guide, Keora. Once back in the spirit world, I realized I had gained additional knowledge, earning responsibility and deepening the color of my spirit. Keora, after his stint as Lance, no longer had to return to earth again. Instead he helped others in the spirit world to grow in wisdom and knowledge.

Returning to the spirit realm, we were purified. As my neck had been severed, I needed to reflow my energy to harmonize my power.

"Theo, in every life, souls return to a planet governed by emotions; there they choose a challenge. Each challenge advances one's understanding so one becomes denser and better able to understand the spirit world's mysteries."

"Can I choose my challenge?" I asked.

"Souls enter an emotional vibration on earth and inhabit humans. They try to maintain the brain's limited logic, create harmony and guide human aptitude to realize their own inherent spirituality. Yet, an ocean exists between the brain's thought and its imaginative control."

"Humans choose, think, and imagine. This makes them ideal to expand their sensations of choice, thought, and imagination, over the senses of touch, hearing, smell, taste, and sight."

"So I have a choice," I queried. Keora smiled.

"As humans tackle a task, their brain analyzes the result, in other words, it thinks. Thoughts create complex pictures inside the brain and direct the analysis. We call this imagination. So if a human controls these thoughts, their imagination creates the correct picture."

"That seems easy," I commented.

"If humanity can prevent their senses interfering, then they produce a defined image, but often their senses overwhelm and hinder the brain, not their intuitive senses. So the brain limits and restricts choice so human imagination remains narrow."

"Is that what I learned being Dion? Learning to rely on my intuition rather than my short-term needs?"

"In part, but you have a long journey ahead before I'll call you an 'old soul.'"

Chapter 2:
I, Theo, hear of other's difficulties.

"Come and meet a contemporary. He returned from an upsetting life experience and needs to rebalance his energy. He had wanted to experience human emotions and their overpowering strength to see if he might limit his brain's logic and judgment."

"He was named Robert on earth. As a child of wealthy parents, he experienced love and devotion because they had but one child to cherish. As a teenager, his friends respected him and often sought his opinion."

"He chose to become a lawyer and his parents supported his education."

"It sounds like an easy life," I said.

"Early on, perhaps, but he was extremely altruistic. He volunteered to teach the homeless to read and write and then gave them wonderful book written by a spiritual metaphysician. The book enlightened them to the power of positive."

"In his thirties, he became a well-known successful lawyer, marrying Lorain and having two children. He carefully selected clients, seeking to defend the innocent. Before accepting a case, he analyzed it thoroughly. Assured of his client's innocence, he forcefully defended their virtue and was frequently successful."

"He was approached by a prestigious law firm to undertake a criminal defense. "We want you to represent our client in court. Your success is impressive."

After examining the evidence, he finally met the accused. Looking into his eyes, Robert knew the man was guilty. He refused the case.

A few days later the District Attorney hired him and assigned him to prosecute the man he'd refused to defend.

Despite being sure the man was guilty, he scrupulously researched the evidence to prepare the prosecution. He was successful and the criminal went into a maximum security prison for ten years."

He told me, "I want to make important decisions and learn about responsibility and judgment because I know the human brain limits logical analysis." He chose Robert's life to give him that experience.

"Robert was fifty-five when that same man came out on parole. Almost immediately, he discovered Robert's office and, using a stolen gun, shot Robert twice in the head."

Chapter 3:

Theo is reluctant to return to the spirit world.

The circle of pain around my chest screwed tighter and tighter, like a vise and then I was dead. I yelled and cried out to my wife, whose tear-filled face loomed over me, but she heard nothing and saw only my collapsed corpse. I was dead.

"What about my business and the house," I screamed. "We didn't discuss what you'd do once I'd gone." Her face was blank, she heard none of my concerns. Could I write to her, I wondered, but my spirit could not grasp the quill, nor would my ghostly fingers write in the dust. She was beyond my help, outside my realm. I had unexpectedly died at age fifty-five. It was strange to be cut off from a life which had been mine just minutes before. Decisions were not mine to take, love was no longer mine to give and receive. I was gone and unnoticed. I had suffered a massive heart attack but after I died the pain was gone. The gate to the spirit world opened and beckoned but I refused to enter. I was in denial, wondering what would become of my body and my family.

I wandered in confusion and sadness. I'd lost my body but remained anxious about its burial. I missed the family I had grown to adore. Finally at the cemetery where my body was laid to rest, I noticed Keora. He was not easy to ignore, pulling me to him, asking me to follow. Uncertain of the path but sure of his friendly guidance, I followed him into a tunnel. Where, as though in an express elevator, the vacuum took us away.

I was confidently at peace— a surfer riding a huge wave. Understanding flooded my physical senses, suddenly hearing, seeing, tasting, touching and communicating with everything.

I sensed every molecule and aligned with each particle and every atom. This was not a physical communication as elements moved inside me and I experienced them within my vibrant energy. I became once again part of the spirit world, a bright color of curious energy. My five earthly senses became one with my soul and I was home again.

In my many life cycles after that, I rarely suffered confusion, so when the inviting gate appeared, I attuned myself to it and wafted back home. Sometimes, I lingered to ensure my earthly family were settled and not devastated. After a few life cycles I learned to communicate to the physical body of humans, not by transmitting detailed messages, but merely sending comforting and warm feelings.

Since human families were often sad and occupied with negative energy, I never found it easy aligning my sensitivities to theirs.

—o0o—

"The spirit world is on a single wavelength. No other force exists but this blissful and singular vibration." Keora explained.

"There is nothing else?" I asked.

"Distractions exist in the human mind making the brain so dangerous but each spirit is a part of the original *one*. For millennia, the human soul has yearned to connect with this singular vibration. As the base of the creator is bliss, feelings and emotions can open the channel to this vibration. Only one power truly exists and that is bliss."

"Why can't humans feel the vibration? It is everywhere."

"Prophets and spiritual leaders guided humans to worship one God and recognize bliss. Physical feelings of negativity are generated by fear and fear is the single enemy. Humans, aligning with fear, block the spiritual strength of bliss. When they cannot connect with bliss, humans align with fear, their minds succumbing to this force. The human mind is perfectly imaginative, creating a bundle of energy, a three-dimensional existence. A human mind so aligned has no limits and then we see spiritual teachers exhibiting extraordinary powers. Every teacher's message urges humans to align with a single power and experience the true reality of existence."

"Why are there so many different beliefs and religious factions?" I asked Keora.

"Humans transform spiritual messages into rules and commandments, creating mythical stories of God and evil. God is the single authority and other energies, like fear, are depicted as evil. The concept of evil is a human creation."

But, understanding this truth in later life cycles, I tried to connect and console my grieving families wanting them to understand I'd happily returned home and their tears were unnecessary. Keora taught me to communicate with my earth family via their dreams because sleeping, freed their emotions making it easier to communicate. It also eased my burden, knowing I eased their sorrow.

Chapter 4:
Soul purification and repair

I did not fully understand soul purification but after my first time among humans, Keora had accompanied me, saying, "You need be free of any damage the world has caused your spirit."

The idea was similar to visiting a clinic or taking a faulty vehicle to a mechanic and I knew my soul needed repair. I hovered as I entered a room lit up with brightly lit particles moving around me.

The room was spherical and waves of light pulled me upward, encircling me. Three healers, behind transparent walls, monitored my health and inspected every part of me. I perceived a shower of energy pouring onto me, as if pounded by cleansing and rejuvenating rain. The energy flowed into me and mixed with my own. My spirit stabilized, making me calm and secure. Even the slight chest pain, caused by the heart attack on my last visit to earth, disappeared and I was harmonized and purified.

The purification revived my memories of the spirit world and my energy. I emerged as transparently white as a young soul in the true reality creation. This was my real home.

Chapter 5:

Reluctance to face the challenge of controlling emotions

My energy color was now a deeper gold but I needed to take on a further challenge. Keora urged me to return and complete yet another cycle.

I didn't relish returning to earth and taking over another life. I loved the peaceful spirit world. Embarking on another role and playing another character, like I was in a movie.

Keora encouraged me to return to earth but our wise leaders did not compel me and always reasoned with me.

"There are no classes in the spirit world but we share a learning environment. The closer you come to the Source, the added knowledge and intensity becomes yours. There is no sequential completion like schooling and college. Rather, energy levels combine and form a chain."

"Understanding in the spirit world helps success and advancement. By increasing your current knowledge, you'll move to a higher level."

"But I still don't want to return to earth and live in a superficial world of illusions. On earth there's too much emotional stimuli and I'll confront human emotions daily." I pleaded.

"Yes, but humans fascinate us because they have choice. Their levels of existence, change their purpose. A spirit soul going to earth adjusts negative attitudes, like jealousy, greed, lack of confidence and so forth, because spirits inside humans easily wander off track and forget their main purpose. Spirits have to frequently return until they attain the highest level. Before souls move to a new body, they experience many classes preparing them for the human's choice."

I recognized the logic of Keora's discourse but did not want to endure another return.

"I don't want to go." I said.

"Look," Keora said, "You have to resolve the dilemma humanity faces with their thoughts, imagination and choices. A soul must take charge of the brain and steer these intuitions. Our experienced guides give us hints to remember when we are on earth. If we go off track, these signs help us regain our chosen route. It's a feeling of *déjà vu*. Occasionally souls lose control and no longer recognize the signs and return unsuccessful. We never blame or condemn. Each soul works with others in harmony and although they might return without accomplishing their chosen challenge, they still gain knowledge."

Sometimes I joked with Keora. "I'll go if you come with me!" But he had a productive role as a guide and mentor and souls on his level rarely returned to earth to help others.

"But the spirit world offers us freedom. I'll leave that behind if I return to earth and meet negative energy and emotion. It requires devotion." I pleaded.

So far I had run away from this but thoughts of returning tantalized me. Earth's beautiful oceans and glamorous nature was also a strong lure. I know the Source had put much energy on the planet to make us feel closer to him despite being on earth.

"I obviously cannot persuade you, but I can tell you how you can help yourself," Keora said.

"The human seeks enlightenment beyond its own existence. This selflessness sets humans apart from simpler animals. Souls, using patience and proven methods, can control the brain. By using source energy and focusing on selflessness, we approximate the spirit world and The Source even the on earth."

"You mean I could feel transcendent, even on earth?"

"It is not easy as the brain transforms human thoughts into images. But, since every thought is energy, an image is merely a concentration that will eventually become reality and matter. So, each human can create a desired image. And this is the secret of creation, which for thousands of years caused wonder."

Keora went on, "Earlier, I spoke of three choices, of thoughts and imagination and their direct relation to thoughts. If you turn thoughts into images they become outcomes."

"Although many humans create outcomes in their imaginations, can they turn these rays of imagination into reality?"

Keora's deft logic, left me wondering this question but he continued.

"The brain is the master of human senses and if humans reach a point where they overcome the earthly senses and let the intuitive senses grow, they focus on their imaginings. They can compress the image's energy into a fourth-dimensional view and thus craft a desired result. This is what humans call meditation."

"Since souls are bliss, stillness of mind is the way to awaken such knowledge. Although most humans think just of their future or their past."

"However there is one moment they can connect with their bliss and find their soul because future and past are not real. The past has already departed and they have not yet created the future. The distance between present and future is plagued with worry and fear as humans often associate the past with regrets and fear the future."

"Many understand this, but preventing humans from learning the magic of creation is their failure in finding their souls. They ignore their control and allow their brains to run them and never reach the pinnacle of the process."

"If humans are doomed to fail, then my task on earth is equally hopeless? Surely?" I asked.

Keora grinned. "I did not say this is easy but the supreme challenge for every soul is make his host body aware of creation and allow the brain to connect the physical world with true reality. If you facilitate this connection, the host becomes one with his soul and enjoys creation. That is your ultimate task."

"The Source is everything and for me as a soul in spirit world, it is indescribable. The Source created us and gave us our own powers but we have to learn to exercise and cultivate that power. We are a sparks and to survive we must develop energy. We must take a physical body, enter its vibration, take over its brain and develop its selflessness.

"Humanity's religions gratify its appetite for selflessness. Saints and prophets attained mastery, and tried to develop systems for their followers. Some lived early in human history and this perhaps explains why extreme control was difficult for primitive societies although their leaders developed rules to follow and encouraged followers to obey."

"Unfortunately, followers misunderstood religious messages and instead of nurturing their souls to develop their potential, they erected places of worship. As their religions grew stronger, their buildings (mosques, churches and temples) became larger and more grandiose. They did not seek to align their energies as their teachers intended but instead, using awe and inspiration, tried to attract believers by building impressive places for worships."

"Keora, why are humans so easily distracted by buildings? Religions seem similar, yet, if an enlightened soul screams its message to foster alignment between spiritual power and their souls, humans worship the body of those prophets instead of understanding their message."

"Enlightened souls want humans to understand their problems, but the worst of all negative habits is fear. It is a rust eating the soul, making it powerless through doubt, insecurity, jealousy, and judgmental actions."

"Look at history and you'll find prophets and saints all shared fearlessness. They never allowed fear to interfere, because they recognized one true authority."

"In the spirit world, we develop our understanding. Our guides teach us to focus the power given by the Source. My favorite exercise is to control my thoughts and manifest them. I make mud. I have exercised for a longtime, and now I've gained added knowledge, I can even create insects under supervision."

"I feel close to the unlimited power and knowledge of the Source. We don't see the Source but feel it, and its harmony brings us closer. When I exercise my creative ability, I feel bonds to my creation. I feel extraordinary developing strong love between creator and creature. I am a painter or composer who creates art or music, knowing the creation is part of, and deeply connected to them. You must understand the Source's connection to all creatures."

"I love the spirit world and its purity. It's a world where energy remains intact and relates in harmony. Each level is dependent on another to advance. In the spirit world nobody blames or judges and no negativity exists. Even if we don't succeed on earth, we are helpfully advised how to succeed. I know you will find the rewards worthwhile," Keora said.

Reviewing my advancement and powers, I'd hoped for more. With added strength I might achieve greater knowledge of creation and grow closer to the Source. Even though I was reluctant to return to earth, the result would be priceless.

As Keora had lectured me, "A brain can be tricky because it can choose. The easiest years are its childhood, when the soul is in charge controlling its moves and choices. The challenge intensifies as the brain matures but the soul not to lose the flow of its frequencies."

In my early lives, I'd sometimes lost control and allowed the brain to lead its own life.

Chapter 6:
Jealousy grows out of control

Early in my spiritual development I needed to subdue jealousy. I took seven life cycles, almost four hundred years, to regulate this emotion. I gained energy in each human life cycle and knew if I returned to earth again, I was experienced enough to control the brain under any circumstance.

In my last life on earth in this series I was Alexander from San Diego, California.

"Well done, Alex your work is nearly as good as your older brother's." My parents always made this type of comparison, leaving me to assume they loved Keith more than me. I became jealous. As I matured, my mistrust of others grew and I sensed they always made comparisons.

At school my teacher acknowledged others and not me. I sought her attention, contriving to make others pupils look bad.

I sat next to Casey in science class. His small flower garden project, overshadowed my model of downtown. I was simmering with jealous rage before he even presented his project. At lunch time, I turned the water on, and left it running in his garden.

After lunch, Casey's project was a flooded mess, the water had overflowed onto books and other projects including my own. Our teacher saw the flooded classroom, screamed and ran for help.

"Oh what a disaster. Turn off the water and rescue what you can." She ordered, running to find the janitor. He and other teachers mopped the floor but most projects were destroyed. Casey was blamed. He was innocent and knew it. But only his project needed water.

He did not return to school for a week. Despite his denials, his parents grounded him, assuming, like everyone else, he was responsible. I never told him I had caused the damage.

In another incident at high school, I was attracted to a blond. She was the most beautiful girl in school. Many boys desired her, but she dated the team football captain. I was on the same team.

Before a championship football game, I put laxative in his water bottle so he suffered stomach cramps and incessant diarrhea before the game even started. He tried to play, but kept running back to the restroom. I wanted to humiliate him in front of the school and particularly in front of his girl.

My malevolent jealousy continued in college where I switched tests papers so my classmates wouldn't score any higher than me. After college my friend Jack helped me get a job.

"We have a vacancy for an architectural draftsman. If you're interested I'll put in a word with my boss." I was interviewed and given the position. Once inside the company, I tried to undermine Jack. He was well-liked, but I coveted his job.

I made deliberate mistakes on architectural drawings, altering Jack's work.

"Can you fix these drawings, Jack has made mistakes?"

"Yes, sir. The drawings must be correct. I'm surprised Jack didn't see his errors."

After three months of my sabotage, the firm let Jack go and promoted me to his position.

I lost control of Alex as his brain overwhelmed his senses and shut my energy down. The only restraint I could use with him was by developing his truthful feelings and warn him of wrongdoings by churning up his stomach. In this way, I forced him to reconsider his behavior, although too often, he ignored me and followed his predictable brain.

Finally, I tried creating intense remorse. I interrupted Alex's thoughts and imposed guilt before he acted jealously and so successfully restrained him. I managed to restrict his jealousy.

Eventually, Alexander changed his mistrustful attitude and gained confidence in his achievements. He made many friends, and they recognized his honesty, self-esteem and confidence.

Chapter 7:
Elders help my choice

Emotions, like fear, jealousy, melancholy, remorse, envy, hatred, dissatisfaction, insecurity, sorrow, and worry swirl around earth like clouds in a wind storm, overwhelming humans who cannot control them. But when the brain restrains emotions, it becomes incredibly powerful.

Old souls attain higher levels but examples abound with prophets like Moses, Jesus, Buddha and Mohamad. Their spiritual strength overpowered the brain's logic, performing miracles, by ignoring the world's wealth and helping others achieve and understand their purpose on earth.

—o0o—

I received many suggestions from our higher and wisest counsellors to return to earth. They discussed with Keora the challenge that would be most effective for me.

They urged me to finalize my choice for another challenge. I was nervous but, desiring more of the Source's love, I did attend.

The circular meeting room was lit with a calming, white and yellow light. On entering, I was bathed in our leaders' positive energy and love. Keora as usual, greeted me with a smile.

I had developed over a thousand years, condensing into deeper levels of color, adding sophistication and overcoming many human flaws but fear was one challenge I had always backed away from. Conquering fear is to battle all earthly emotions in combination of negativity.

"By selecting this challenge, you will endure dramatic emotions and battle harder than ever with the human brain's reason." One of our leaders said.

"You also need to confront love." He said. "It is charming and colorful, but can be dark and scary when aligned with fear."

Fear and love were my challenges.

Finding a life depended on many aspects, especially when some souls choose emotional lives, making their tasks more difficult.

One of my contemporaries chose to become disabled person, a victim of a house fire who'd thrown himself from a third story, suffering first-degree burns and damaging his legs. He was compensating for a previous incarnation as a cruel military commander who'd burned villager's houses, and broken fleeing occupants' limbs.

Chapter 8:

Social obedience and its consequences

My Spiritual vigor and the diversity of my human lives, meant I experienced contradictions. In one life I'd abused women and harassed them, but then returned as a meek young girl, growing into a shy and biddable young woman in an impoverished family.

In another life cycle I'd chosen to be a woman, born in London. My mother birthed me in her room and had the local doctor attend as it was much cheaper than a hospital birth. She lost much blood in labor and took weeks to recover. My father worked as bookkeeper and, as his wage didn't cover our expenses, my mother also worked as a maid.

I arrived one month premature. After examining me, the doctor had pronounced,

"She is healthy but small and weak." Since my mother was frail and unwell, my father's sister looked after me for a month until my mother regained strength. My father was very proud of owning our house. It was small and Victorian with kitchen and living room downstairs, with two bedrooms upstairs. The staircase and bannisters were wood and at every step, it creaked as though the house might come apart. The downstairs floor was dark stained wood and in the corner of living room a big fireplace made the house cozy and comfortable.

My father, with help from my uncle George, had built that fireplace. A big window looked on the neighborhood's busy streets. My mother decorated the window with a beautiful, hand-crocheted curtain, screening our living room and providing privacy from the busy street.

My uncle George, a creative carpenter, had helped my father build our furniture. He even built our beds and dressers.

Before I come into their world, my family had endured a disastrous ordeal. My mother became sick from consumption and spent time in hospital. The cost was very high so my father borrowed money from his employer, using our house as collateral. His wage was too low to repay the debt and he had no choice but to send my eleven year old brother to a friend in the north.

After my mother recovered, her old job at the local grocery store had been given to another. Uncle George had rich acquaintances and introduced my mother to the owners of a large house where she worked as a maid. I was born in the middle of these problems.

My older brother, Jim worked as a farm boy in the northern England, earning enough money to attend school.

As a young girl, I was shy. After I'd learned to talk, I understood my parent's tight budget, often making it difficult to provide enough food. Every morning before going to work, my mother dropped me at my aunt's where I played with her son, Henry. In the evening, she picked me up. My parents disliked the arrangement, but had no choice if they were to make ends meet.

At my aunt's house, I realized I was out of place. She did everything for me just as she did for her daughters but feeling I was a bother, I sat in a corner playing with my doll, JoyeeJoyce. My hardest time was lunchtime where I shared their meal, believing I was an imposition.

In my lonely moments, playing alone, speaking and crying to JoyeeJoyce and complaining I wasn't with my parents, my aunt was extremely kind and sometimes, noticing me crying, hugged me in her soft, white arms, and cried with me. She treated me as if I was her own, but her husband, Robert was not the same. If he was home, he only paid attention to my cousins, playing with them, as though I was not there. He had a big fat belly and a baldhead. As he played with my cousins, his belly wobbled like gelatin and that made me laugh.

In contrast my father was thin and tall and with neatly combed blond hair. He was clean-shaven except for his mustache.

"My mustache is important and shows my importance." He combed and brushed it in front of the mirror every morning. He wore a dark black suit and a tall hat every day. I loved to play with his suspenders, wrapping them around me.

"You are a very handsome daddy," I told him. "I love you very much." As he shaved, I looked up at his face, and, only reaching his hips, I noticed how tall he was. As he shaved, I played with his shaving cream and put it all over my face. Imitating him.

My uncle George helped pay for my schooling but I was not part of the crowd and kept to myself, having few friends. Other children rarely asked me to join their games. Playing team games, no one picked me for their team. My shyness intensified and I lacked confidence.

My brother Jim briefly returned home when I was eleven. He had finished his schooling and was as handsome as my dad. He went to India, learned business and eventually traded with merchants around the globe.

My parents' finances had stabilized and my father managed to pay off his debt. My mother no longer worked out and instead cared for our family. Our house looked even better due to my mother's extra attention and her appearance improved as she wore nicer dresses and looked after herself.

After school, I practiced piano and read poetry. I loved music and my mother encouraged me. Although a piano was expensive, my uncle George built one and had friend help with the internal structure. My father often asked me to play before dinner. He thought it was very good form in society for a lady to play piano. It showed she was from a good family and of a better class. By then I was well aware of my father's obsession with class and society and its opinion on him.

Despite the good things improving in my surroundings, I still had little confidence and was extremely shy. I rarely voiced my opinion and accepted all that came my way, complying with contrary opinions to avoid attention.

My parents had concerns about my future and as society dictated young ladies should marry, my father focused on that point. I was not interested in any man and I didn't look for an involvement. My mother had taught me to manage a household, and how to cook. I hoped to enjoy my life as it was, not wishing to marry, but my parents' insistence was high. They feared people's opinions and their sarcasm. I was too shy to meet anybody and had little confidence about my appearance. I was unaware my long and wavy blond hair, big whimsical blue eyes, feminine curves, full hips and a rather spectacular bust, were beautiful.

In the mirror I saw a weak and ordinary body, and sensed I was too introverted to socialize. Walking on the streets, men tried to accost me and gain my attention, but I kept my head down and timidly walked at a distance from the crowds.

One day, walking home from the bakery, I saw a shadow behind me, and approaching. I increased my speed, keeping my head down, watching the shadow closing behind me, almost touching me. My heartbeat was so strong that my entire body shook.

A rough but friendly man's voice called my name, "Janet." I stopped, but still kept my head down, too scared to look up.

"It's me Billy, your brother's friend, remember me?" Reluctantly and fearfully, I looked up, recognizing Billy, a good friend of Robert's from the farm in northern England. He was big and strong but with a large belly. He was balding and his yellow teeth made him appear ugly. I winced at his bad breath.

"Hello," I said, trying to walk around him.

"Wait," he said. "Let me help you carry your bags. A beautiful lady should not carry heavy bags. What am I good for then, beautiful?" He moved his hand toward the bags, trying to touch my hand while taking the bags. He bent lower, staring into my face as I fearfully looked at my feet.

"Relax, if you'll let me, I'd be honored to walk you home." With his rough voice and a big ugly smile, he went on, "So, how about it? Shall we?"

I didn't want people see me with him on the street. Our neighbors were narrow minded and seeing me with Billy, they would have started a rumor. My father was too sensitive about what people might say.

I shook my head while still looking down and timidly replied, "No, no! It's quite alright! Thank you Mr. Jamison, I'll carry my bags. Have a good day," and politely bowed my head in goodbye. He stepped in front of me and with every step his big belly wobbled. He kept insisting rudely, and being very shy, I finally acquiesced. He took hold of the bags and sized me up and down. While walking he bumped against me, touching my back. As we walked, I smelled his foul breath. He was the first stranger who'd come that close to me. I was shaking and afraid. I walked fast to reach home as soon as possible.

His licentious eyes scanned my body and I sensed the image forming in his mind. He looked pleased with himself, kept talking and asking questions while I walked faster, ignoring him. We arrived at the small park near my house and headed across it. The sun shone through the gray London sky spreading its calming warmth, I trembled with anxiety and felt as cold as ice. I tried to walk faster, but he kept up, trying to slow me down.

"Why don't you slow down, I want to talk and get to know you, Janet? I've always liked you and you're beautiful. Why not let me look into your wondrous blue eyes?" He jumped in front of me, making me stop.

I was panting with fear, his face was so close I smelled his foul breath on my cheeks. As he came closer, I retreated with my hands in front of me, indicating he should stop. I stepped back, bumping into a tree, looking left and right, no one was nearby and the surrounding bushes kept us out of sight. I'd taken a short cut and walked into the middle of bushes. He put the bags down, with his rough left hand touched my neck, putting his other around my waist.

I was shaking like a leaf with my heartbeat pounding. I needed to scream, but was too timid to even raise my voice. I couldn't look at him and lowered my head. As he touched me, his breathing got quicker and excited. He rubbed against me, licked my neck, trying to kiss me. I couldn't say a word, as he put his grubby hand into my blouse and fingered my breast. I pushed against his sweaty chest, but he hung on to me. I cried silently, frightened someone would see us. I didn't want to disappoint my parents, but felt helpless. One of his hands was in my blouse and the other inside my skirt touching me. Suddenly, we heard voices approaching. He removed his hands and adjusted his dress. He picked up the bags, pushing me forward to walk. I was shaking like a small bird in snow and couldn't feel my steps. I walked and he followed.

I thanked God for the voices that stopped him, because I was too shy, weak and fearful to do anything. Nearing my house he cleared his throat, tilting his head closer to me, lowering his voice, he said, "Janet, I didn't mean for what happened back there, it was not what I wanted, but I feel different around you and can't hold back. I want you Janet. I want you every day. Let me be your man. I want to marry you and make you my wife." My heart almost leapt out in anger but instead I walked away even faster and ignored him. He came up and angrily said, "Wait, I said I'm sorry Janet, but if you talk to anyone about what happened today, I'd be very upset, you understand? You keep this between us, okay? Now here are your bags, take them home but I'll see you again."

Tears streamed down my face. I was as white as a ghost and scared as a rabbit.

I did not tell anyone, but the memory ate my insides, making me weaker and weaker. I wanted to tell my parents but lacked the courage. My confidence evaporated. I could not even look at myself in the mirror.

I did not wish to go on living if I had to suffer this way. I was shy before this, but afterwards lost my remaining confidence and could no longer stand up for myself. Every time I went into the city, I feared seeing him again.

Whenever I cut across that park, my fear, the thought of seeing Billy and the memory of his violation tore me apart, making me want to run and cry. I hated him. I wanted to scour my skin where he'd touched it. My disgust was so strong, I couldn't bear to touch my own body. I went to bed clothed, not wanting to see my own naked body. Days passed and I felt a little better, trying to forget that day. Sometimes I thought it had been a bad dream or a nightmare. Despite my superficial recovery, I stayed fearful and lacked confidence. I was sure I'd carry those fears with me all my life if I couldn't change.

One day soon after, returning from my daily shopping, my father opened the door dressed in his formal attire. I knew we had a guest in the house. I went straight to the kitchen and then heard the familiar and frightening voice of our guest. It was Billy. He sat with my father, while my mother served them afternoon tea. I was breathless and shaken by the renewed images of that dark day, I was devastated.

My mother called, asking in her polite and kind voice, "Janet, why don't you join us? Mr. Jamison has honored us with a visit." I couldn't reply. I didn't know what to do. If I ignored her and ran to my room, my parents would want me to explain and I couldn't tell them what had happened. If I walked into the living room and faced him, I was not sure how I'd react. I was totally confused and that was combined with numbing fear. My mother called again, "Janet, Are you there dear? Your father and I would like you to join us and Mr. Jamison and for you to please play the piano." She implored.

Involuntarily, not wanting to disappoint my parents, I went into the living room. He sat on the chair, legs crossed like a gentleman, wearing a suit, looking shaven and presentable. But his grimace revealed his true character.

"Oh, Janet, how lovely of you to join us! Have you met Mr. Jamison? I'm sure you two know each other." My mother spoke formally.

"How do you do?" I turned, trying not to look at him.

I asked my mother to forgive me and excused myself for not playing the piano. My father defended me, asking my mother not to force me. I was glad she didn't, because I was too upset to concentrate. After few hours discussing politics and sport and business with my father, Billy left, but he'd made a good impression on my parents. That evening, my mother kept talking of his handsomeness and gentlemanly qualities.

Every time she mentioned him, my stomach churned and I nearly vomited. Finally she said, "Mr. Jamison is fond of you. He's very pleasant and would make a good husband. Perhaps you should learn to know him better?"

I'd suspected something, but not this. A few days later, as we sat together, my father, pouring himself a brandy, turned to me, saying, "I think Mr. Jamison is going to be your future husband. I approve of him. I just invested money in his merchandizing and that will help provide for your future. He will make you a good husband." My father wore a satisfied smile on his face.

I had not spoken out before and always accepted my parent's opinion, but now without any hesitation, I screamed, "Stop this! I don't want to marry him. I don't want to get married at all."

My parents were shocked, looking at me as if I was an alien. My father, raising his eyebrows, said, "Young lady, you're out of line. You will marry him. I know what is best for you and it's time you married. I'll ask him to formally present himself to you. Your mother and I expect you to be reasonable. Now good night."

That was the extent of our discussion. Billy was an uncouth pig but I was too weak and couldn't fight. I failed myself and married him as though I had no choice.

As Janet's soul I didn't want to fail but had to stand up for what was spiritually and ethically correct. I needed to prevent Janet's mind, overcoming the dutiful acts her brain commanded her to obey. I must be a powerful subconscious and direct her brain's false illusions or I would fail and come back to earth again and inhabit another life.

After the church service, the guests, relatives and witnesses gathered for the wedding feast and celebration.

I sat on my husband's right, but smelled his foul breath and heard his open-mouthed sloppy chewing throughout the feast. I pasted a smile on my face and turned it toward the guests, my parents, my uncles and aunts and my new husband.

"Where will you live?" My Uncle Peter asked.

"We have rooms over my husband's warehouse," I replied. "We will stay there until Billy's business is better established."

He nodded his head sagely, "That makes good sense. Don't spend money until you've made it." He smiled to the other guests, a satisfied cat celebrating his wisdom.

"We're looking forward to grandchildren," my mother remarked. Billy circled his strong arm round me and squeezed.

"You'll have no worries on that score, mother." He laughed loudly and then belched, also loudly. My mother covered her face with her hands, looking embarrassed.

I was required to dance with Billy. The fiddle players and drummer played a slow reel and we staggered onto the cleared floor. Billy was so drunk, I supported him but he still had his lewd appetites, leering suggestively, clasping my bottom and grinding his big belly against me.

"I waited a long time to get you in bed, little darling and see you with no clothes on. You needn't hide your beauty from me."

I blushed, looking at my feet. I dreaded being alone with him and did not want to look at his hideous grin, or inhale his disgusting breath.

My father was a welcome relief as my next partner, smiling to the guests in proud satisfaction as we danced. I sat down after that and watched Billy drink and drink. He clasped my wrist with his free hand and wouldn't let me leave.

"Let me go and prepare for our nuptials," I urged.

"No, you sit beside me. I've paid a lot for your company and this is our wedding day." I turned my pasted on smile but recoiled at his grotesque and lascivious leer. I knew this night would be the worst of my life.

Eventually, and at the urging of Billy's friends, "Go on Billy. Pretty soon you'll be too drunk to perform." We lurched out of the hall with Billy almost crushing me as I supported his weight.

My mother and I had set up a modesty curtain across one end of the bedchamber. A place for me to change and wash. Billy collapsed on the bed and I went behind the curtain to remove my gown and don my shift.

"Come out," he growled. "You're not hiding back there. I want to look at you. All of you."

I gulped with surprise, nearly running away in fear, but forcing my feet to obey and trembling, approached the bed.

"That's better. I want to watch."

My trembling fingers, stuttered over each hook and eye, playing waiting games around each bone button, but eventually my gown dropped to the floor. Billy had loosed his own breeches and his fat hand delved into his linen.

"Take that blouse off and then come here. I want to suck your teats."

I realized I was an animal to him. I did not have breasts or a bosom, but teats like a farmyard animal. He pulled himself upright and dropped his breeches. His linen pushed out hard and I saw he was aroused, just like a bull. I took off my blouse, exposing my breasts. He was dribbling with desire as he grabbed me, putting his vile lips on my nipple and sucking. He buried his other hand in my linen and within me. I shuddered but remained still.

He stopped slurping on me, looking into my face.

"You don't know how much I want you. It seems I waited an age." He undid my linen, dropping it to the floor. I kept my arms beside me, although I had a desperate urge to cover myself. The lust in his eyes was a hard beam; he threw me onto the bed, burying his manhood between my legs. I squealed in pain, but he thrust harder, tearing and ripping me. He imprisoned my arms above my head and slathered his mouth around my breast. He panted harder and harder until he groaned like a boar wheezing its last breath. Trapped beneath his inert weight, I finally wriggled clear. I put on my shift before sliding into the bed. I was a ruin as I saw my dreams fade like an abandoned crumbling church. In the next weeks I tried being a dutiful wife but he drank every day and after eating the evening meal, he forcefully took my body, using it as he wished. He watched me naked, forcing me to dance, compelling me to stroke and kiss him. I never loved him but would not oppose my husband. Although, one evening, feeling tired, I said, "No, not tonight."

He looked at me, as though he was a wild bull. "I say when I'm having you. You're my wife. You have a duty!" He tied my wrists, bent me over the table, pulled up my skirt and shift, lashing me with his belt across my buttocks. I refused to scream and give him any satisfaction, but wept quietly into the table. Having whipped me into submission, he abused me from behind.

I couldn't tell anyone. I was too shy to tell my parents and embarrass them for my marriage failure. I knew I had let them down; my marriage was my fault. I thought of killing myself but knew this was the greatest sin and a feeling of optimism gave me hope to go on living.

My mother's wish came true when I became pregnant. I did not want his child within me, I would be birthing a devil. But knowing I was pregnant, he did want sex and left me alone. Pregnant I was safe. My mind changed regarding the baby, looking at it as my angel of salvation. He still expected me to work around the house and in his warehouse but I was pleased he needed nothing sexual.

I escaped every Sunday morning to church. Billy did not accompany me.

"I work hard all week. I need my day of rest." Although Billy's spiritual guide was to drink all day, starting just after breakfast. I was four months pregnant before I met Albert at church. He was twenty-eight and in the military. He was very handsome and his uniform emphasized his good looks. He was a gentleman and became a friend, although he knew I was married. Whenever I looked into his brown eyes, I saw worlds to discover.

I feared Billy would find out, no matter how innocent our friendship. The thought of discovery scared me, increasing my anxiety. But, whenever I saw Albert and looked into his light brown eyes, I confided in him and our friendship grew.

I looked forward to Sundays and seeing Albert. I was happy and calm gazing into his eyes. He was always polite, charming and intriguing. Our friendship was my solitary hope, other than my child, that offered protection from Billy's abuse. Albert was attracted but disregarded it, knowing I was married. Looking into his eyes, I gained confidence and eventually shared my feelings and fears, telling him about my abusive marriage. After I told him about my suffering, he softly wiped the tears from my cheek, held my chin and kissed me. Confirming our loving togetherness.

As Janet's soul, I was excited whenever she saw Albert. I transferred my excitement to her brain, blocking its logic, so she began to imagine and stand up for herself. Albert's eyes were the sign guiding Janet closer to him, as she gained confidence in his deep affection. Every time, she saw Albert, I diverted her attention to him, making her forget her insecurity and directing her into happiness.

I guided Janet to avoid wariness and timidity and to accept Albert. Eventually I completed my mission, overturning her fears and transformed her into a confident woman.

Billy's business took him away from the home, delivering goods to outlying village stores, so he occasionally stayed overnight in an Inn. He had once used a carter to deliver these goods, but growing mean and greedy, decided to make these deliveries himself.

He drove the wagon, sometimes in the severest weather. One day, when the ice and snow sparkled in the weak winter sun, a constable knocked on the door.

"Are you Mrs. Jamison?" he enquired.

"Yes, what is wrong?"

"Madame, I have bad news. There was a wagon accident on George's Hill, just outside the village. The wagon and horses skidded on the ice, overturned and crashed at the bottom. The driver, Mr. Jamison was killed. The horses were so badly injured we shot them too."

I was stunned. I was suddenly a pregnant widow and almost collapsed. The constable sat me down and made tea.

"Can I let anyone else know?" He asked. I thought quickly.

"Yes, can you tell my mother? She will come and help."

Finishing his tea, he replied, "Certainly Mrs. Jamison."

I told my mother all I had concealed. I slowly grew confident, after enduring Billy's tyranny and the ordeal faded into in my memory. I had a beautiful loving marriage with Albert; he welcomed our son Roy.

Chapter 9
Choosing another life

We referred to it as the 'deciding' room. The wisest souls selected a few lives we might inhabit on earth. I reviewed them and one caught my attention. I couldn't see every detail, but merely the life's overall picture. The details of a life are put together by the wise ones, but can be altered depending on how a soul, controls the brain. Choosing is like watching a movie, we observe lives and feel them in an instant.

As a soul, taking over a life it is imperative we do not underestimate the human mind and its ability to choose. The human mind's choices alter the life and its entire mission. So not only has the soul a mission to accomplish, but also must keep the chosen life on track.

Most of the time, we experience many life cycles before succeeding since humans frequently deviate from their destined path. While souls work on advancement, our memories of the spirit world are blocked and we forget the spiritual world while on earth. By forgetting our past, we rely on the human brain and concentrate on making direct connections with the brain.

Inexperienced and younger souls are blocked from any knowledge of the spirit world because its influence can be misused, especially as an immature soul cannot control the brain.

Only advanced souls hold memories of the spirit world and retain signs and hints to bring them back to their original purpose. As an advanced soul, my memory allowed me control and eventually helped me overcome fear. I'd be aware of my presence in my next body at all times.

Providing signs and reminders is an incredible assistance from the higher powers as they help us overcome the brain. In my life as Janet, the sign was Albert's eyes, letting me defeat her brain's negative habits.

In my life as Janet, I'd gained much karmic strength giving me an advantage for my next life.

—o0o—

I chose to be a successful entrepreneur in southern California, who had everything, especially an abundance of love. His struggle was the fear of losing love.

My advisor covered the common considerations. Since I was a mature soul, he mentioned using my power and its allowable limits. He told me my memories of the spirit world would not be blocked but cautioned against using supernatural powers, warning me to care for the precious body I'd inhabit.

Everything was ready for me to visit earth once again.

I was not changing my mind. Returning to earth, working through the habit of fear, would bring me closer to my creator and his deep knowledge and love. Despite leaving my beloved spirit world and giving myself an emotional challenge on earth, I decided to complete my purpose, hoping to overcome my challenge in a single cycle.

I knew Keora would watch my every move and the spirit world was supportive as I set out. Before leaving from the transportation gate I received empowering love and extreme confidence.

Sophie, a contemporary, reminded me to visit earth's wonders while the baby of my body remained inside my mother, reminding me to breathe the pure air of the Pacific and watch the beach sunsets for her.

I looked lastly into Keora's eyes, feeling his trust and pride. He embraced me, imparting his strong drive.

"My spirit will protect you like a blanket along the way," he said.

—oOo—

Chapter 10:
Birth

I arrived on earth as an embryo in my mother's womb. I was free to wander as a bird, as long as I left behind a little vitality to help the baby survive. I'd promised Sophie to absorb the view of a beach sunset in California. Hovering on the Pacific's edge and feeling its dynamism, I saw the Source's work in every particle.

I traveled to many places and met other souls along my way. Some in transition and others returning to the spirit world. Some were enjoying earth's beauty in spirit form before involvement with a physical body. I enjoyed this period, controlling my energy and sensing perceptions without the five limited human senses.

I sought total command of the human brain. This was a perfect opportunity to face my challenges, of both fear and love. Fear was the stiffest challenge, but as long as I controlled the brain, I knew everything on my path would be illusory. If I aligned with the brain, then I'd retain mastery. I didn't tell Keora because using my soul's abilities was contrary to spirit regulations. But, by dominating the brain and moderating it, I'd not only enjoy my time on earth but also complete my challenge.

—o0o—

In the deciding chamber before my departure to earth I chose a particular baby because of its wealthy surroundings and whose father, a diplomat, frequently traveled to Eastern Europe. The mother was a celebrity's daughter and a fashion designer, living in Los Angeles, California. In all my lives on earth, the City of Angels was my favorite city.

I was their child after five years of marriage. They had been pressured by parents for grandchildren, but after moving to California, and in the fast lane of success, they decided to have a child.

Two weeks before my birth in December 1962 my mother was excited. She had monitored her health, being careful of what she ate and ceased smoking as soon as she realized her pregnancy. My father traveled a great deal but arranged his schedule to spend time with my mother. They worried about my health and worried whether I'd have all my fingers and toes. As the time for my birth neared, mother spent time resting. I did not leave the babies body as the due date approached so I'd focus on controlling my human brain.

The exciting day for me to have a fresh adventure was at hand. Instinctively, I hoped to emerge from her womb quickly. Her muscles pushed me forward. On one hand I was afraid to enter a world of limits and illusion but on the other I had my spiritual power and used it to make everything easier. I stopped resisting and let her muscles move me along the birth canal with every hard push.

Suddenly, I saw the light of the world, my first glimpse with my baby's sight. I was scared and confused. The closer I came to the light, the less I felt my power. I found the brain's activity too vigorous to stop Yet, I needed the discipline, but couldn't get the level right, constantly losing the brain's changing frequency. I experienced the first sign of human emotions, and grew very scared. I had not expected to endure these feelings again.

"Oh God, hate, anger, fear, doubt, sadness are combining with love, happiness, and confidence—the sensations are overwhelming. With my level of expertise, I thought I'd be in charge. I want to return to the spirit world. Keora, Keora help me, I want to return."

The room was blindingly bright and I closed my eyes. The doctor cut the umbilical cord, my physical connection to my mother. I was bursting with emotions and let out a wail. A nurse took me from the doctor, cleaned me and wrapped me in a towel. She looked into my eyes before handing me to my mother. She exclaimed, "Oh thank the lord. He's a healthy and beautiful boy."

My mother held me tight as if I was still part of her. She kept kissing me, telling me she loved me. My eyes began to function and I gazed with rapt attention at my mother's face and blue eyes. Her soft lips smiled, making me feel at ease. I reached out to touch her lips, I closed my eyes but did not sleep. The strong connection to my mother was a pure feeling of magical love. She closely examined me, adoring each tiny finger and toe, and kissing me over and over.

With each kiss, a startling vibration of emotion entered my nervous system and went directly to the brain. My mind translated this as good passion and sent it to the heart. At last I regained some order in my spiritual role of battling the brain. I tuned into a mellow and adorable frequency sending love to the heart.

I monitored the brain's every wave. I had not expected all these emotions at the same time and grew tired dealing with them, especially as the brain acted on pre-programmed commands, as though I was not there. Despite my advanced level, I had difficulty controlling the brain. I refused to give up and did everything to conquer this challenge. Then I realized, by using my spiritual vitality on the earth in its three dimensions, then I'd transform it into four dimensions as it was in spirit world.

Examining my thoughts I saw this would not make me stronger. My incarnation on earth was to increase my knowledge, test my strength and grow my energy. I couldn't ruin my opportunity by cheating. I wished for Keora's supportive enthusiasm, I wouldn't give up but needed help.

—oOo—

Chapter 11:
Life as a child

"Let's call him William," my mother announced.

"Why William?" My father asked.

"It's a strong name. I believe he will be strong." She said. My father smiled and agreed. They hired a middle-aged lady to help run the house. She had kind familiar eyes and whenever I looked into them, I grew extremely comfortable, wondering if Keora was watching over me.

Keora knew I needed support and I assumed it was him. I was closer to my spirit world yet to completely enter human life, it was essential I adapt to the body and release the spirit world. Most souls regret the decision to return to earth and take time to grow used to the body's continuous growth.

The caretaker often looked after me and I observed Keora's will threatening to overwhelm me whenever I looked into her eyes but knowing Keora was there encouraged me to focus on the body and exercise control.

I grew quickly. My brain, hungrily soaking up knowledge like a sponge, made it harder to restrict the brain's vibrations. Every second, millions of cells replaced old ones, shaping the growing brain. If I meddled, it changed its frequency, allowing the brain to use its own wavelength, ignoring mine.

I maintained its growth while adjusting to its frequency. Every time I saw my mother, my feeling of joy turned into deep love – a comfortable and reassuring sensation but lurking behind it was a hidden fear. I thought of love, without a guarantee of its continuity, and dreaded love fading away. I tried not to let my fear interfere with my joy and love for my mother.

—o0o—

I know fear arrives in one of two ways. I can fear gain or fear loss. When humans desire, fear arrives, creating paranoia and hesitation. Or fear grows stronger when gaining a desire, but then fears losing it. For example, I feel deserted if I assume no one loves me but if love comes, I also fear losing it.

—o0o—

I adored my mother's beauty and cradled in her arms, touched her full red lips, the charming dimple in her cheeks, and played with her long blond hair until I fell asleep.

Whenever my father held me, telling me he loved me, the feeling was different from my mother's but the same frequency. The feeling was comforting but held a hint of fear. Each of my parents had a different vibration for their love. The more I sensed love, the greater I liked it, but I feared it too, forcing me to wonder why fear interrupted a sensation so deep in my core.

Feeling love, amazed by its sensual vibration, fear ran inside me like an electric current. My fear of encountering that fear was painful, because if I didn't constrain the brain's frequency, then my connection was diverted. Fear obstructed me and re-routed the frequency, leaving me powerless over brain and body. It was a sudden reaction, but I resisted.

By the age of four, I controlled the brain and remained in touch with the growing nervous system. If I did not manage its control, I'd easily lose the wavelength. Therefore I divided my effort and communicated with the body as an imaginary friend. The other half of me maintained its course of brain growth. I even told the baby my name in the spirit world, Theo.

We grew closely acquainted as I, Theo, became his friend. He told his parents about having Theo as his friend and playing with him. They, thinking he had an imaginary friend, didn't adversely react while the world viewed me, Theo, as William's make-believe friend.

His mother often joked using me, Theo. One night, encouraging me to brush my teeth, she pretended to brush Theo's teeth. As William, I believed her and it was very effective. Theo was also reassured, knowing his own mother saw him as William's pretend companion.

Establishing Theo as William's friend, a very strong bond formed between us. Having trust and confidence in

Theo eased up William's mind and I easily took charge of the brain's responses.

Chapter 12:
School

At the age of seven I started school. I did not like leaving my mother and nanny. My mother was my favored companion. I felt out of place on my first day, depending on Theo. Other children stared while I played and talked with Theo, my imaginary friend. They thought I was weird and kept their distance. In the first few months I made no friends and missed home and playing with my mother. Once I enrolled in school, my parents dismissed my nanny.

Theo and William were in tune and William depended on Theo who directed his conventional behavior or he wouldn't participate. William's parents grew concerned because his imaginary friend affected his school social life. They'd thought Theo temporary when I was younger, but now I attended school, it was unacceptable, especially as I talked and played with a person no one else saw. For William to be accepted, I, Theo, tried to phase out my appearance as an imaginary friend and worked on his thought and brain patterns.

Decreasing Theo's drive toward external stimuli, brought it inside William and I experienced all his heightened emotions. As William experienced differing stimuli, his heart rate varied. Every emotion changed his pulse and all parts of the body felt the effect.

If I was scared, my blood pressure lowered, chilling me. I tasted bitterness as the amygdala nuclei in my brain (it processes emotional reactions) utilized hormones to balance my heartbeat.

But I was weak and powerless to prevent my response to my parents. Every time I saw them, my heartbeat increased, increasing my blood pressure and my anxiety. Muscles tensed, producing increased levels of serotonin. My eyes softened and the moisture inside the pupil increased. My lungs expanded and even my nostrils inhaled extra air. I became alert but also happier.

But feeling this love, I greedily sought more and more but if those for whom I felt love walked away, I worried lest I lose them. My distress took over, my heartbeat increased and anxiety built. In turn my body produced adrenalin and noradrenalin but only after the adrenalin rush burned off, did my moods mellow and relax.

The brain did this without my interference. It automatically stabilized my fearful reaction and so I let it work and be a powerful ally in controlling my fear.

I remained unsure why I was scared immediately on the heels of feeling love. When younger this worry was not apparent but as I grew my fear of love grew beyond restraint, interfering with every bodily function and blocking my communication with the brain.

I adjusted to my surroundings in our rich family life. As I aged, I enjoyed having my wishes gratified whether in toys, books or treats. I was not enthused to return to earth, but when my wishes were fulfilled, I was satisfied and encouraged.

I enjoyed my friends in school, my teacher encouraged my talents and the results pleased my parents. Yet, despite attending one of the best private schools, where the pupils were all from the same social class, I had a sense of foreboding every time I looked at my mother, feeling her enveloping adoration. Our bond was strong and had been since I'd nestled in her womb.

Before leaving for school, I carefully examined her face to carry that image for the whole day. My strong feelings were tied to the anxiety of losing her some day and the shadow of the ugly cloud never left me.

As I grew to adulthood, I worried I'd lose touch with William. In other life cycles, I had not been as advanced and powerful as I am now and had not managed to limit the mind's power, especially after entering adulthood. At my latest level, I overcame certain feelings, was empowered and maintained my force without emotional disruption. It kept my life in harmony and happiness. But I wondered what would happen as I matured.

Chapter 13:
Gilda

I met Gilda in my third year of school, she arrived mid-term as a new student. She kept her head lowered, her golden curly hair obscuring her face and rosy cheeks. She smiled with blue eyes, walking to her assigned seat. I examined her every move as she walked by me. She sat two seats away and I had a perfect opportunity to study her. As I stared at her, she looked back at me. As I looked away, she smiled. The image of her smile remained in my mind.

At our mid-day break, I looked for her. Dave and Dustin, my best friends, wanted me to play basketball, as we usually did in recess. I ignored them as if I had not heard them calling my name. She sat alone, eating a green apple, watching other kids play.

I thought to say hello, but my legs were powerless. Looking at her, was the same as seeing my parents. Cheerful and joyful feelings transformed into love. I had not appreciated those feelings except for my parents. I forced myself to overcome my doubts, stepping closer to her.

"Hi, my name is William. You are the new girl?"

"Yes, nice to meet you. I saw you in my class; you sit two seats away."

I was overjoyed she recognized and had noticed me in the classroom.

"Where did you go to school before?"

"In Washington DC. My parents moved to LA for business. How is this school? Is everyone easy to get along with?"

"Well, I am. Our teacher is good. Some students are difficult, but mm... Yes, we are all friends. Do you enjoy basketball? We could go to the gym and join Dave and Dustin. What do you say?"

"I'd rather stay here. Maybe later. Do you like painting? We can color. I have books and have the best one with me. Here, sit down and I'll show you."

I virtually abandoned my other friends in favor of Gilda, who soon became my best friend. Other children made cruel and harsh jokes about me being a lady lover, but I didn't care because the time I spent with Gilda was magical. We spent all day together and the joy I knew and the laughter we shared were better than the sports I'd previously played. Her blue eyed smile, like that of an angel, made me want to be with her every moment. With her, I was content, joyful, happy and childish. Yet somehow I still feared uncertainty.

In 1973, I turned eleven and Gilda helped my mother organize a surprise birthday party. After school I walked home with Gilda.

Gilda gave no hint of the surprise waiting for me at home. I'd asked her to stay for the evening, so we'd celebrate my birthday together.

"I'd like to stay and help you celebrate. I wouldn't want to miss your birthday," she said.

As I pushed open our gate, I saw an ambulance parked by the main door. We ran up the steps to the door. My father was in the foyer smoking. I was surprised to see him this early in the day, he often barely made it in time for the family supper. As soon as he saw me, he bent forward, holding my shoulders and tearfully hugged me.

"Your mother is not well." I looked over his shoulder and saw the balloons and decoration she'd put up for my birthday and did not understand.

"I want to see my mother." I said angrily.

"A doctor is with her. We just have to wait here William. Why don't you and Gilda go and ask Mrs. Pennero for something to eat? I'll call you when you can see her."

I was upset and worried. This morning she'd been fine, kissing me happy birthday as she'd handed me a sandwich for lunch. I wondered what had happened. Sighing, I looked at Gilda and we went to the kitchen.

On the way, I overheard a maid say, "…she's been ill for a long time and the doctor is not very hopeful."

"Poor Mrs. Oakley. She's grown weaker over the past two years. What will happen to young William?"

"He had no idea his mom was sick. He'll be shocked if anything happens to her."

"What will happen to my mom Mrs. Pennero?" I demanded.

"Oooh, William, nothing honey, come and sit here. Hi Gilda how was school? Would you like something to eat?"

Something was wrong because my mom had been sick for two years and they hadn't told me. How come I hadn't noticed? She always looked beautiful and was always kind to me. I never saw weakness or sickness.

"I'm not hungry, Mrs. Pennero. Why is my mother sick? Will she be okay? Is she going to die?" I asked.

"Oh William, don't worry yourself. She'll be fine. Here, why don't you share this spaghetti with Gilda? I know it's your favorite."

I wondered what they did not tell me. I wanted truth and, as her son, I deserved it.

"Gilda, I'm going to see if mom is okay. Do you want to come?"

She hesitated but shrugged, indicating okay.

My father was not in the foyer so I headed for mother's room to see for myself.

"Let's go upstairs Gilda!" As I'd climbed the stairs, I thought of my beautiful mother, imagining her in front of the mirror, combing her blond hair.

Her door was ajar and I heard voices inside. She was in bed under a blanket. The doctor adjusted her IV drip and two nurses, as well as my father, hovered in attendance.

"Mom, are you okay?" I cried in a panic.

My dad ran to me, held my hand, and took me to her. She looked peaceful, but her spark had left. Her blue eyes were blurry and her face looked sallow. She turned her head slowly, as if in pain, and then smiled.

"Oh baby, how was school today? Happy birthday my little man. Don't worry, dad will tell you what is going on. I'll be fine in no time…"

She coughed, the doctor put his hand on her shoulder and urged her not to talk. I didn't believe she'd be fine and knew she'd leave us. Gilda was beside me and held my hand firmly. She stepped away, pulling me to leave mother alone. In my room we sat on my bed and sadly looked at each other. I knew I was losing someone dear. My love for my mother was leaving. I had dreaded this moment. Gilda sat beside me, trying to ease my pain.

She stayed the entire night holding my hands, hugged me, lying beside me and comforting me.

—o0o—

My mother died from blood cancer – leukemia. She died on the anniversary of my eleventh birthday. She'd expressed her love for me until the day of her death.

I didn't cry but was afraid. I'd known that fear whenever I gazed at her. I sensed the same fear when I'd first seen Gilda. Every time I loved, that worry grew stronger. I was afraid of one day losing the love.

Eventually, I understood that fear lurking behind the love. The more I sensed this fear, the more distant I grew. I didn't want to celebrate my birthday ever again and looked back on that day remembering only my concerns lurking behind love.

I was lost and disappointed as thoughts of my mother filled me with mournful agony. I was depressed but Gilda kept me going and I became almost as attached to her as I'd been to my mother. The horrible memory of losing my mom was an atrocious reminder of the pain of loving and losing a dear one.

Chapter 14:
First love

I changed with hair growing on my chest, under my arms and in my groin. My voice deepened and my body shape altered. Urges and feelings I'd not known before took over my body and mind. This period was crucial as I, Theo, had to maintain harmony within the brain but I used my knowledge as a progressive spirit. The body created hormones and the brain re-configured but I couldn't lose control.

William's logic remained in my charge but if I was to remain in control I needed to manage William's emergence into adulthood.

My physical appearance had changed rapidly. My brain sent messages to nerves and glands, sending hormones rushing through my body. I loved the feelings, so reminiscent of unrestricted emotions in the spirit world. I embraced the sensual urges and stopped interfering and even encouraged them. Strangely, these new senses intensified around Gilda, leaving me vulnerable. Other females did not arouse the same reactions.

I was too young to have intercourse, but I didn't want to block my urges. I stimulated the brain, creating sensuality, like an addict. I grew close to the freedom of the spirit world whenever I experienced these desires. To boost these feelings, I stayed around Gilda. She noticed and experienced her own attraction.

"I feel desire when I'm with you, but it's empty because I cannot do anything with it." She told me.

"I want to touch you and caress you. It's very sensuous but we can't indulge these feelings." I replied. We did not act on the sensual feelings, but as we resisted, our desires grew stronger. I needed Gilda like a thirsty man needs water.

Wisely, her parents didn't let her spend nights at my home. I'd spend days with her day but it was always difficult to say goodbye. We acted like lovers in thought if not in deed.

Gilda matured into a beauty. Her face and body matched her exquisite angelic attitude. Concealed inside her was the softest and most forgiving heart. She turned her talents into painting. Her work was as innocent as her pure and immaculate heart.

She hoped to bring peace to earth. I laughed and teased her about her pure intent every time we spoke about it. I told her she was naïve to ignore reality and we argued and fought over our differences. I did not ask to see her disappointment and hated to hurt my softhearted angel.

I was determined to maintain and increase my father's wealth. I was not selfish but enjoyed my experiences on earth. I couldn't understand Gilda's desire to help people in need.

This discussion frayed our relationship but I did not see how this hole would become a tear no tailor could mend.

—oOo—

Nearing the end of our high school days, I waited for a letter of acceptance to college but Gilda surprised me as we sat by the pool drinking.

"I've been accepted into a human rights course at George Washington University. I'll leave Los Angeles before September." The news burst from her lips, she was so excited.

The sky collapsed, crushing me.

"What? When? What do you mean? We didn't apply for DC. We applied to college together. I don't understand!"

She pulled out her acceptance letter and said,

"I didn't tell you William but I didn't apply to Berkeley. I sent my application to George Washington. I know we argued about me trying to change the world, but this is my life's dream and I won't ignore it."

A flood of tears threatened to burst from her gentle blue eyes. Thoughts flashed through my head but I couldn't piece them together or make sense of them.

I was Gilda's best friend but she had selfishly hidden this from me. I had never understood the seriousness of our discussions. I thought her hopes were a childish fleeting dream, which she'd grow out of. I'd never thought it a strong a belief or perhaps I'd ignored the truth.

Our arguments had been scissors shredding our friendship, tearing us apart. I'd ignored her desires to keep her closer to me. I wondered how I'd missed her sincerity. Why did I not see her yearning until now? She would not be at my side if she went to Washington DC. Gilda was the girl in my life. Every moment of my life belonged to her. I saw and sensed her presence, even if she was not beside me. I sensed her full lips on mine, her curly blond hair falling across my face, her soft small hands touching my cheeks, and her innocent blue eyes gazing at me. I loved her with every breath.

Anger, frustration, upheaval and confusion overflowed within me. But these emotions become one, that of fear.

Angry I had pushed her away from me, but I knew it was too late to change her heart. I didn't know what to do or how to make her stay. I was heartbroken at losing her but also mightily afraid.

—oOo—

My emotion poured into me and blocked my mind. I lost control because William's emotions outpaced me. I stood firm, but my entire messaging with William's brain was cut and I let him down. William became a physical human, using my energy to survive, relying solely on his brain for logic. William's fear buried him and I was paralyzed by his overpowering emotion.

Chapter 15:
Depression

After she left, I was helpless. Feelings I'd fought to overcome in former life cycles reappeared, asserting their influence. I became skeptical, doubtful, paranoid and angry as my life seemed meaningless. I barely slept and when I did, suffered terrifying nightmares.

I skipped classes, staying in bed, sorrowfully reviewing my memories of Gilda. I had no tolerance for idle conversation and even kept a distance from my father, locking myself in my room.

Two weeks after her departure, Gilda phoned. Her calm voice eased my agony but she sounded different and I realized we were already strangers.

She bubbled across the phone line with news, of her grandmother, the fun she had with her new college friends and changes in the city, but never once said she missed me.

I replied I was fine and busy with my friends but realizing we no longer shared feelings, I was keen to say goodbye. The woman who'd once understood me, seemed distant and I feared sharing my emotions and telling her how much I missed her. I was scared to love again. I felt betrayed and my feelings for her turned into doubt and disbelief. By loving her I had opened my heart and life to her. I was broken and after that phone call, our last for some time, I understood what I felt for her was wasted.

I was not into making new friends and just wanted to get on with my college life. My anger seethed just under the surface. My youth, wealth and authority sucked me into the three-dimensional world. I was led by logic, not my heart, as I cynically viewed all others as untrustworthy. I encountered many girls and explored my sexuality and enjoyed physical contact but I'd shut my heart down and was inert inside. On rare occasions turning up a flame of attention, was nothing compared to my feelings for Gilda. No other woman gave me the same feeling.

Chapter 16:
Success - alone

After college I entered the world of business and became a successful investor by buying small struggling companies and merging them into my own corporate entity. Some small companies, lost their value but a few had huge growth potential and with a small investment became strong stock leaders. I took risks but soon became known as a powerful and knowledgeable investor in these ventures.

Some companies had no chance of survival and I sold their stock options to make a profit. I hated doing this as the fate of the employees was in my hands. The employees trusted me, but quickly discovered their companies were closing and they'd soon be out of work.

But, for those unfortunate companies, I created a division to which unemployed staff submitted applications and, using my human resources, helped them find jobs within my organization. If they needed additional education, my company funded fifty per cent of their tuition, promising employment after graduation.

My peers claimed this money was wasted but I viewed it as an opportunity and after several years my corporation had a corps of loyal employees who greatly increased our profits so I never regretted my decision.

Gilda still haunted me. I went to bed hoping she'd return to me, it was almost ten years since we parted. She worked for a non-profit organization in Indonesia. She wrote infrequently, asking about my life. I didn't share my feelings but wrote back detailing stresses of my everyday business life. I still recall, opening her envelopes and smelling her wonderful scent and running my fingers across her writing. I kept her letters in a box and looked at them daily.

Usually, just after my morning coffee, I opened the box and inhaled her scented letters. A few times, I'd boldly asked of her amorous life. She gave few details but I gathered she would not live with anyone else and become emotionally involved.

I nearly told her my love remained beyond description but trying to express it, my fear and vulnerability choked me into silence. I could not admit feelings for Gilda, or change my life by joining her, and was petrified of commitment. The thought of her leaving again, paralyzed me.

Even the pen in my fingers quivered whenever I started to write a sentence admitting my thoughts. The pen took control and stopped me writing.

Although distance separated us, I pushed myself closer to her beautiful face thinking of her every day – she was healing medicine for my stress and anger.

Closing my eyes at night, her beautiful angelic hovered behind my eyelids. The more I looked, the more a spark glowed within. It was powerful and buried inside me.

—o0o—

Chapter 17:
Re-awakening

In September 2004, I was pre-occupied by a company takeover. I kept a close eye seeing an opportunity because the directors of a pharmaceutical company had rejected their own chairman thus making it vulnerable to its investors. The concept of acquiring it in a takeover intrigued me. I knew other companies were looking at this opportunity but I hoped my bid would be successful.

The day dawned sunny and warm. I drove to work, reviewing the speech I'd written for my negotiations. The hot cup of coffee I carried added to the heat and made me feel overwhelmingly hot.

Emerging from the elevator I sensed a familiar calm. I inhaled, letting it wash over me. Nearing my office, a scent dazzled me, transfixing me. For years I'd been addicted to the scent from Gilda's letters.

She stood inside my office, gazing out of the window. I gasped, completely mesmerized. Long dormant emotions ran through me, overwhelming me.

My joy and excitement replaced all my feelings as I hugged her. She was more beautiful than I remembered, her face had matured, but her innocent blue eyes still gazed with gentle kindness. I thought I'd burst with joy. Gazing at Gilda, I was speechless and didn't know where to begin.

I had much to tell her and much I needed to hear. Ten years without her were desolate and empty compared to my rich emotions. I wore my passion on my face and could not hide it.

I was complete and contentment shone in every fiber of my being. I promised to share my feelings with her and tell her how much I loved her and had missed her.

—oOo—

As Theo I was awake again. Years had passed and I'd been powerless and dominated by the mind. My victories only occurred if William concentrated on his love for Gilda. I wanted to be part of him again but whenever he'd experienced guilt for even thinking of Gilda, his fear and anxiety pushed me away.

Gilda's visit changed William's emotions and, I reasoned, if love brought fear, then love would defeat it.

Although I had minimal charge of William's activities and thoughts, I was hopeful I'd regain control because every time he sensed Gilda's love, he opened his heart.

Strong positive thoughts made me an important part of the subconscious and visible to him. If he admitted his love and submitted to it, he would permanently defeat the fear.

I hadn't forgotten my purpose and my spiritual role. This was my fight and my challenge.

I had conquered many challenges in life cycles on earth. I'd previously mastered and restrained the negativities surrounding the brain.

But fear is the mother of negative senses. The brain was logical and pictured a limited three-dimensional image, seeing every image as a physical experience. My strength was the power of water, washing stones and turning them into sand, gradually, but inevitably.

The brain recognizes right from wrong by its logic but I understood comprehensively and in greater detail. I saw wrong and right by understanding the future. This is why in the earthly world; people doubt. While those who have overcome the five senses, and the limiting reason, are always certain of their decisions. I had waited ten years to incite William's passion for Gilda.

—o0o—

I had dreamed of this for ten years. In my excitement at seeing Gilda I forgot my takeover meeting. My secretary paged me, warning me I was already late but I said to her,

"Cancel all today's appointments and reschedule them." She stared at me in confusion, picking up her phone, as I returned to my office.

Gilda's perfume softly teased my nose, relaxing me. She had clipped her long blond hair and her face was a radiant diamond. We talked for hours and it seemed unbelievable how ten years, filled with many incidents and changes, had passed so quickly and almost unnoticed.

We lunched nearby on a delightful restaurant patio. Talking of her job in Indonesia, she almost burst with pride and joy. She had three months off before she had to return.

Not only did I listen to her soft calming voice, but gazed at her lovingly, adoring her every move.

I was delighted, despite our years of separation that she'd chosen to spend her free time with me in Los Angeles. When I asked her,

"Why are you here after so many years?" She merely smiled.

"I waited until you were ready to see me." She said. I didn't fully understand her meaning but was happy she was beside me after ten years. Her smile reminded me of first seeing her in the classroom.

From that day forward my life was Gilda. I gave my power of attorney to my legal counsel so I could spend my time with her. In three months she'd return to Indonesia, unless I could change her mind. My love was thirsty and nothing quenched it. Every time I saw her, my urges burst through my skin and pushed me closer to her.

I became different inside like I'd returned from the past, a shadow of familiarity and companionship. I'd found a long lost friend. Because of my love, the feeling flourished and I nurtured it. The more I bore, the greater was my unlimited power.

Alone, I closed my eyes and entered a serene world behind the curtain of dark sight. I focused, trying to see in the bright tunnel of light. I saw myself as a child with no worries. I recalled my long lost imaginary friend Theo.

He'd never left me. I heard him trying to reach me, but I couldn't hear his words. I focused on the glorious light, recognizing his friendly face with its warm smile and wonderful vitality wrapping my body. I reacted as though wanting to leap out from my bones. My joy was indescribable and I almost forgot to breathe. I didn't want to open my eyes and lose Theo.

Whenever I gave my attention to other problems, I lost Theo. But as I thought of Gilda, Theo's reflection reappeared and overcame it. My love for her brought Theo closer. Whenever I thought of her leaving, Theo disappeared and unease and worry built, making me afraid.

I didn't know what I feared but it was similar to the fear I sensed loving my parents and the same fear I attached to losing Gilda. I wondered why, whenever I desired love, this horrific worry followed it, making me fearful. I knew that Gilda's strong love weakened my fear.

—oOo—

I brimmed with happiness to see William finally recognizing me, Theo, as integral to him. Seeing me, he was joyous and Gilda's love was our path to communication. It was my task to propel him away from his fear of losing her. I hoped his faith in Gilda would overcome his fear of losing her. His adoration of Gilda was the storyboard, on which his biography would be written, and the story would evolve around Gilda who he'd never leave. Hopefully his fear of losing her would vanish forever.

I stretched for the brain's nerves and frequency, as I'd never previously done. I used all my resources to control the mind. I was Theo, I was William, and I was in charge.

Chapter 18:
Testing choices

My world changed after Gilda returned. I no longer cared for my surroundings as long as I was with her. Like an addict, I needed my daily dose of her sweet kisses and the feel of her hands around my neck but grew anxious as her departure approached. She'd asked me to accompany her and experience her life. I was almost convinced, but reviewing my life and my business, her offer seemed pure fantasy.

Although with my wealth and connections, I'd be a wonderful asset in her field. She told me how people in Indonesia did not need of money, but needed attention. They needed care and support from other human beings instead of being crushed by the global economy. She wanted me to work with her, hand-in-hand and said, "If you don't like it you can always return to California."

I shook my head, "Look around, my life is immersed in business. I cannot just leave it." But in truth, I didn't need to stay in California as I was rich and had enormous power, I could live anywhere. But, changing my life was scary and I didn't like it. I thought about going with her, wondering, all the time, if I had enough courage for such a dramatic change. It meant putting my life on hold just to be with her. I doubted I was strong enough to commit to Gilda's dream.

I had too many doubts even though this was a golden opportunity to confirm my feelings. I also had my good friend Theo to consider. He was connected to loving Gilda but suffered with my hesitations. My decision would prove what type of person I was.

The takeover deal was half completed and it needed my final guarantee. I had scheduled a meeting with the board of directors in two weeks, where I would speak and sign the agreement. The directors expected my personal attendance and commitment.

I did not ignore Gilda, despite the importance of the meeting, but was glad she was with me, but grew anxious about her leaving. I was afraid of how I'd react with her not there. She was adamant for me to accompany her. I didn't want to go and begged her to stay. "I need to make a difference in the world," she said. "This is vital to me as a human being!"

Her dreams of making change had not altered even after ten years and we'd argued the same point before and it hurt me even then.

She wanted me in Indonesia to acknowledge my commitment to her. She needed to confirm my sincerity. If I went to Indonesia I'd demonstrate my loyalty, and affirm my devotion. She knew I loved her, but was unsure if I'd go out of my way to prove it. It was not a test or trial, but an affirming gesture.

I asked her to marry me and to stay in Los Angeles as a demonstration of my commitment. I declared I did not want to be a minute without her and would be devastated if she left.

I hoped she'd stay with me and keep my life unchanged but I was not prepared to abandon everything to gain Gilda's trust. I was neither strong enough nor brave enough to change.

Three nights before Christmas she left me in sorrow and loneliness. I hoped she'd change her mind at the airport and stay with me. I'd have married her if she had stayed. I told her so, she smiled and kissed me. I was too blind to realize she needed me to commit to her.

She hoped I'd change my mind and waited for me to buy an extra ticket but I didn't because I was afraid. I didn't want to change my life and my excuse was the vital meeting scheduled for the following week. A voice screamed inside me, saying. 'do not to let her go,' but I didn't listen.

My brain told me to wait until the business proposal was settled and that she'd return soon, but my heart throbbed with worry, crying out, "Don't let her out of your sight again!" My heart begged me to react, but my brain refused, asking, "What about your meeting? You can't go to Indonesia!"

"Why not?" my heart replied. My reason controlled my thinking and would not permit me to leave such a promising business behind. I tried to sort out my worries as my heart grew anxious. The hardest moment was our parting as she turned and walked away.

I'd seen the pleading and kindness in her eyes combined, as it was, with her disappointment. My lack of audacity, my lack of will to change and be spontaneous saddened her. My heart nearly jumped after her. I lowered my head in anguish watching her leave. I couldn't move and closed my eyes so I didn't watch her leave.

I turned into myself as she walked away, but even with my eyes closed Theo cried and shouted, "Don't let her go!" I tried to reason that Theo was not really there and he was just a hallucination. I reasoned Theo was a figment of my imagination and appeared because I was sad to see her go. I turned around, not looking back, and walked to my car.

Driving home, I could not concentrate. I didn't hear the wailing horns as I drove slowly. Her beauty stayed in my head. I saw her teary eyes begging me to go with her. I pulled off the freeway and stood on the roadside feeling drained and lethargic, but brimming with disappointment. Closing my eyes and rubbing them, I saw Theo holding out his hands and pleading with me to go after her. I stared carefully at that blurry vision that was no illusion, but real. Theo moved further and further away replaced by the dark shadow of fear. I didn't want to open my eyes and lose Theo but didn't know how to save him.

I shouted, "What do you want me to do? She is gone!"

I heard an echo inside me, "Go after her, now!"

That echo resonated inside me, opening my eyes as I looked fearfully around. My hands shook and I trembled. I needed to follow her. Suddenly, realizing my business deals did not matter, I craved to be with Gilda and prove my love to her even if it meant burning up my wealth. My purpose in life was to show Gilda I could not lose her even if I circled round her like a moth around her candle. I did not fear burning in her flame because she was the purpose of my every breath.

I took the freeway back to airport praying to find a flight. I abandoned my car at the airport doors, running inside like a madman and demanding a ticket to Indonesia.

"I am sorry sir, all flights are full. We have a seat on December 26 but just before Christmas is our busiest time." This was the last thing I needed to hear. I needed to get to there, but how?

I called my secretary to arrange a flight on the company jet. She called back, "It will take until midnight before it'll be ready to leave." I was like a child having a temper tantrum, if I'd been in my office, I would have fired everyone. I screamed on the phone, "Get it done. I will not tolerate any delays. I'll be at the boarding gate at midnight." I calculated I'd arrive in Banda Aceh, Indonesia at six pm the next day after an eighteen hour flight. My mind ran in circles. Outside, I didn't see my car and assuming it had been towed, took a cab home to shower and pack.

The evening was dark and rainy and a brisk cool breeze chilled me. I arrived in plenty of time but inside the terminal, my pilot looked frightened. I guessed there were technical issues. "What's going on?" I asked.

"We can't get clearance for take-off because of this stormy weather."

"How long before we can leave?"

"I don't know. We just wait." Then, surprisingly ten minutes later, he told me we could board.

I tried to sleep on the long flight. Surprisingly, upon closing my eyes, I didn't see Theo.

But I was perfectly calm and serene and didn't have to close my eyes to feel it. I experienced joy, happiness, and confidence. I was relaxed and devoid of anxiety.

We stopped in Osaka, Japan for few hours. I hadn't reckoned on this re-fueling stop and it made me impatient.

In the morning an item on TV caught my attention. News channels reported weather warnings around Indonesia and Thailand. No matter what the weather, it was imperative I get to Gilda and let her know how much I loved her. Listening, I worried for her and her safety.

I looked up and saw my pilot. In a hesitant voice he said, "Banda Aceh airport is closed." I jumped up, but weak from lack of food, I was dizzy and everything went dark.

I came to with the pilot helping me sit down.

"They just told me Banda Aceh was hit by a tsunami. Many people have died… Everything is flooded! We have to land nearby. We'll find the closest airport and from there you can drive inland. It may be difficult as everything is underwater and roads are filled with wreckage. I don't think you can easily get to where your lady is."

"Just land and get me close to Banda Aceh. I have to be there. No matter what!" We boarded quickly.

I tried calling Gilda on her cell phone but she did not answer. I even called her mission but there was no response. I was agitated and sat in the airplane hoping to see her soon. The plane bounced up and down in the strong winds and I grew dizzier and weaker as the storm intensified. I had no appetite as my craving was to see Gilda's blue eyes again. I drank coffee to stay awake while staring out of the small window looking at my reflection. I was tired and worried, but was not afraid and regretted nothing.

The sky was clear but rain was imminent and the wind was extremely strong. I had arranged transportation and immediately got off the plane and into the car. Most roads were covered by water. The driver spoke in Bahasa Indonesia on his radio and told me we shouldn't head anywhere near Banda Aceh. I repeatedly told him I must be there despite the cost. But just a few kilometers from my destination, the road was blocked to traffic.

The driver took me to a small hotel. I kept trying Gilda, and finally her answering machine kicked in, but there was no room to leave a message. I'd traveled almost 9000 miles and was stuck a few miles from her camp. The camp phone did not work and I assumed the tsunami had destroyed the phone lines.

I wondered how to get news of her, or to her? How to tell her I came after her? I wanted her to know how much I loved her and would marry her even if I stayed in Indonesia for the rest of my life.

I stayed at the hotel overnight, continuously sending text messages to her. The tsunami's aftermath was shocking. The hotel opened all its rooms for survivors and offered extra beds in every room. I shared my room. Everyone was emotional with stories of loss and death. Beside me an Australian was searching for his brother. I loaned him my cell phone to call his family. Everyone cried, uncertain of what to do and where to look.

I kept calling Gilda but there was no answer but found a number for her co-worker. It was too late to call, but with all the commotion, I couldn't wait another day. I wanted Gilda to know I was in Indonesia and had given up my business life to be with her. I needed to see her smile and feel her warm hand on my face. I longed for the touch of her soft lips. I needed her beside me.

The phone rang and rang but after four rings, just before I was about to give up, a lady's tired voice answered. I introduced myself, apologizing for calling so late. "Can you help me find Gilda," I asked. "I am just few miles away staying in a hotel. Do you need help? Is everyone okay?"

There was silence on the line and I thought I'd lost the connection, I repeated "Hello, you still there?" She replied, "Yes, I'm still here, maybe I should meet you. I'm close to where you are."

"Oh, okay. That's fine. Is Gilda with you? Do you need a car?"

"No thanks, I'll be there shortly."

She hung up. I was excited thinking I'd be with Gilda soon.

Chapter 19:
Grief and loss

I was standing under a covered porch when a car pulled up and two people got out. The sky was dark and the moon hid behind dark rainy clouds. I was excited to see two people and tried to see Gilda's beautiful wavy blond hair in the dark and rain. I grabbed the handle to open the door and the gusty wind slapped rain onto my face so I couldn't see clearly.

As they stepped onto the porch, I saw two strangers under the weak light of a small yellow bulb. I introduced myself and shook hands. I'd spoken to Rita on the phone and she was accompanied by Andrew. He was dressed casually, was sunburned and spoke fast with an Australian accent.

Rita wore a mud splattered raincoat. She had a strange look in her eyes, but I couldn't grasp its meaning. I immediately asked when we might leave to see Gilda. Rita and Andrew exchanged looks and were silent and uncomfortable. I repeated my question and asked, "Is Gilda okay?"

Rita replied, "Mr. Oakley, don't panic. She was involved in a terrible accident after the tsunami hit where she was working. She was badly injured and the locals took her to the hospital. We were lucky they found her among thousands still missing. She is in hospital."

"Will she be alright? Which hospital is she in? Why didn't anyone call me? What happened?"

"I'm very sorry, but she was working as the tsunami hit. Gilda and others were in a house as the roof collapsed. They were all badly injured. She was taken to the hospital and is in bad shape, but the doctors think she'll make it. There are many people missing and we've been helping survivors and transporting them to hospitals. We also take names of the survivors and distribute them to safe points and camps. This is terrible and horrific. I have seen too many dead people and some have died in front of me and I couldn't help them." She cried, continuing, "We had no way of contacting you. I understand your feelings. Please stay calm and we'll take you to the hospital. I called you from there earlier."

I grabbed her and held her in my arms to calm her down. I asked her if she needed any water or food. Although I knew food was scarce and many were devastated by what happened. Both Rita and Andrew's clothes were covered in mud and stained with blood.

The image of my beautiful Gilda under the rubble horrified me. I was in a nightmare. The sound of crying babies brought me back to reality and I asked if we might drive there.

I was shocked and in total disbelief. I found it hard to believe my Gilda was seriously hurt. Oh my sweet Gilda, How did I let this happen? If I had been there it might not have happened.

I grabbed my raincoat and jumped into their Jeep and we drove to the hospital. Two other men joined us to ride to the hospital to find their families. I was amazed that despite the disaster, people kept up their hopes. Hope gave them strength. On the dark drive to the hospital, there were flashlights and so many people searching.

The hospital was just a few minutes away. The rain poured down, adding to the rainwater left over from the tsunami. My Gilda was close the whole time I had been looking for her. The Jeep barely stopped before I jumped out and ran into the hospital.

I was in the middle of chaos. There were hundreds of tents and camps, people running around and more injured being brought every minute. I didn't know where to go. The people searched the lists on the hospital walls for survivors. Children, wearing nametags, gathered waiting for help.

Inside was busier than the outside with sounds of pain, mixing with loss and sadness. The doctors and nurses were running. I saw a nurse running on the other side of the corridor. I grabbed the stretcher she pushed and helped her move it to the main rooms. They had put beds on both sides of the corridor while stretchers lined the floor. The nurses tried to attend to everyone but needed more help. There were so many injuries and only God knew which were the worst were and which patients needed immediate treatment. I stopped a nurse and asked Gilda's whereabouts. She pointed to the names beside each bed. The staff had no time to help and left me to find Gilda myself.

I didn't waste a second and searched the names. There should have been just four patients in each room, but each room was crammed with patients. Some rooms contained twelve patients.

Rita and Andrew were behind me. I heard Rita's voice, "Mr. Oakly, She must be in this room here, Hurry!"

My Gilda was in the corner, wrapped under a blanket with an I.V. on the back of her hand. Her face was pale and badly bruised. Her eyes were closed, and she had a bandage around her forehead and injuries over her body.

I grabbed her cold hand and kissed it. My eyes filled with tears but I called her name softly to see if she was awake. She responded in a weak voice, uttering my name and turned her head to see me. She smiled but was in great pain. She closed her eyes again. She was in very bad shape. I ran outside, yelling for a doctor.

The doctors and nurses were all tending others.

Everyone was rushing around trying to help. Then I saw a doctor, ran to him and asked him to help my Gilda.

"I'm sorry there are other patients more critically injured." He pushed my hand away, saying, "I'm sorry." and moved on. I was desperate and didn't know what to do. Even if I arranged transportation to a larger city I was afraid it would be too late.

"Rita, Gilda is in a bad way. Do you have any doctors on your staff who might help?"

"Yes," she replied. "That's why Andrew came, he's a physician."

He was already checking her file and examining her.

"Will she be fine? I kept asking him. He didn't reply, but continued his analysis. He opened her eye to examine it. I saw her blue eye, but there was no awareness, warmth, or spark. She had passed into a coma.

"She has numerous fractures and needs an X-ray but she has internal injuries."

"What can I do? I'll do anything."

"She is in-line for surgery but her internal bleeding is extremely serious."

Even if she was transported to another hospital, the closest hospital was miles away, and there was no guarantee they'd operate. Andrew looked to see if they might port her into surgery immediately. Nurses helped Andrew pushed her bed into the surgery waiting area. It was crowded with patients, with babies crying and patients screaming in pain.

Gilda did not awake. I held her hand and kept kissing her face.

"I love you Gilda. I cannot survive without you by my side. I'll give up everything to be with you." I longed to glimpse her kind blue eyes and feel her warm hand on my face.

Then she coughed and, looking at me, said faintly, "William, I love you, don't leave me … I love y…" She then closed her eyes.

I shook her and kept calling her name but she did not respond. I screamed for help and Andrew joined me by her bed. Two other nurses pushed me aside to check her condition. Andrew said something in Bahasa and started CPR. I kept shouting, "Don't you let her go!"

He kept pumping her chest, forcing air into her lungs and checking her pulse. Everyone waited to see movement or any change. Then he stopped, checked her pulse and said, "I am very sorry, but she is gone."

—oOo—

Chapter 20:
Nearly losing William

They covered Gilda's body with a white blanket. I cried and wanted to scream. How could I live without her? I'd shaped my life around her. I'd tried everything to be with her and changed my life to be closer to her. The world was unfair. Why was she dead? Why was she gone? Why did I have to be without her? Why did she leave me? It was not fair! I had altered my life and now she was gone. I wondered why being in Indonesia was so important to her. Why couldn't she stay in California and marry me?

I complained out loud for being alive without her. I knelt beside her bed and let my anguish out. I screamed and cried but no one heard my voice. Tears poured off my cheeks, my mouth was open and I needed to scream, but I had no voice. After a few seconds, I gasped, inhaled and then heard my sobbing. Andrew held me back, trying to calm me, but I craved to touch Gilda's body and not let her leave me.

Suddenly I was giddy. I lost all motivation and my world went black. I tried to stay standing by Gilda's bed, trying not to fall. I couldn't keep my eyes open but resisted very hard. Finally, closing my eyes, I saw my old friend Theo. He appeared sad, disappointed and helpless. The same feeling coursed inside me. I wondered if he was my soul. Was he a reflection of myself? Seeing Theo, I was calmer as I had a shoulder to cry on and wanted to be with him. I didn't resist further and let myself go.

My knees buckled and I crashed to the floor. I was still hoping Gilda would return to life. She lay on the bed like an angel. Looking at her beautiful face, I knew her spirit no longer inhabited her body, I had lost it.

Gilda was gone. My body lay on the floor senseless. I had no feeling, no ambition and my heart barely beat. My existence seemed meaningless and empty. It was a void I could not fill. I was still alive, but powerless. I had lost my essence.

Everything around me fell into two dimensions and my brain agonized putting everything around me in order. I had memories without feelings. I was a lifeless empty shell. My bones and muscles had no purpose.

Andrew ran to me. Put his hands on my chest, pushed me forward and checked my pulse. I had no memory of him and did not understand our connection. My brain, distorted by the lack of control, barely analyzed or even comprehended movements around me.

Opening my eyes, I saw light and surrounding images, but couldn't connect to them. On closing my eyes, I saw empty darkness. I was missing my soul. I was alive but without a soul, my body had no meaning.

Semi-conscious on the floor, I looked up to Gilda's body. She was not in the hospital bed any longer, but above me and communicating. My body was limp and I was unable to move. In effect, my brain was dead, but yet alive physically. I had no strength to try and understand.

My internal energy was calm and without emotion. My instinct blocked my senses, forcing me to look up, to feel her love, her spirit, her soul touching my hair, kissing me and telling me she was fine.

—o0o—

As Theo, I knew William was a wreck. Every inch of his body was filled with Gilda's love. From the moment he faced his fear and followed Gilda, he overcame his fear. My purpose was accomplished and I wouldn't let him stay in this three-dimensional illusion anymore.

I saw Gilda's spirit radiating but different from other spirits I've known. Her spirit was covered with layers of love. She looked glorious and she astonished me with her extraordinary beauty. I have not previously encountered such strong love and radiant intensity. Her liveliness was an enigma. All my time on earth, I'd thought she was an illusion and another tool to fulfil my purpose. I'd used her love to accomplish my mission. I would not have thought Gilda's feelings were so real. How might I see her spirit?

She was not an ordinary soul. Her spirit was beyond exquisite. I desired to join her and communicate with her but I needed to close William's emotional channels. I had control over his body and shut his mind to a minimum, keeping him barely alive, with minimal and basic bodily functions. I was in love with Gilda. My adoration was not limited by the world as her affection coursed through me.

She energized and purified me. I begged her not to leave and to take me with her. I needed to be with her and feel her wonderful love and her reality in the spirit world.

I wanted to worship her existence and make love to her. I'd never known such supernatural power in any of my past lives. It was the first time I became aware of the emptiness when she was absent. I couldn't go on without Gilda.

Her love was so powerful, I was alive as a soul for the very first time. As she joined me, she asked for my patience and tolerance until I saw her again in spirit world. I didn't want her to leave but as she entered the exit tunnel, my strength dissipated. The further away she moved, the weaker I became until she was gone and I was powerless. Since I controlled the brain, I left William's body and reached out to Gilda's soul.

As I exited William, I returned to the spirit world. I was happy, calm, and relaxed without the senses of the human body. I felt great and kept searching for Gilda's soul. I found it hard being without her beautiful and powerful devotion. I looked down and saw William's body on the floor and Andrew running toward it. I realized it was not my time to leave William's body, but wondered about my feelings for Gilda's soul? If I returned to William, I'd lose Gilda and have to wait longer to rejoin the divine power. If I didn't return to William, although I'd have accomplished my mission, I would not have completed my cycle.

Disappointed I called for Keora.

"Please return me to William." I cried, disappointed that I needed Gilda, pleading to join her special appeal. Keora was in front of me but I could not see him. I was a soul and out of physical body, but sensed his calming influence. I saw Gilda's soul, but could not visually connect with Keora. I comprehended his presence, but couldn't see him.

Keora knew, seeing him would make it unbearable to return to a physical being. He was a wise teacher and asked for my patience.

I looked up hoping to glimpse Gilda, before searching for the way home. I had authority and experience, but only William's life cycle would lead me to my real home. I gave in to that thought, knowing that being William was my path to see Gilda again.

Once joined with William, I was shocked with electricity shock but jerked and everything became normal again.

—o0o—

Andrew was bent over me and, as I finally moved, he stopped performing CPR. With my soul once again in place, I sat up and tried to stand. My brain attempted to keep up with these changes and my heartbeat became so strong, my body shook. I gathered myself together and looked around to grasp my surroundings.

For the first time, I completely felt myself. I was not scared or frightened. I was connected to a strong being inside me. An entity or instinct gave me that feeling. I clearly visualized such a powerful force whenever I closed my eyes and saw Theo, my old imaginary friend. He was my protector, not separate as we shared an identity. We were one.

Chapter 21:
Utopian life (?)

For the first time in my life I was fully integrated and no longer calculated things around me and did not analyze life. I sensed things and looked at people dispassionately, seeing imaginary friends inside them. I didn't care whether rich or poor, illiterate or educated, disabled or healthy. I only saw the honor in their hearts. I was not scared even in the middle of night to go to a dangerous neighborhood, I just saw the purity and adulation inside each person. The feeling was overwhelming. I was in a four-dimensional frequency and living another life.

Money had no meaning, nor was the life-style important. I was intrigued by calmness and serenity controlling my every move and thought. My brain did whatever I asked. It made me see my intuition and my bliss. Feeling this way, I could not survive in the materialistic world and with that insight, knew I should be away from any human culture.

Having such a view, I saw the world in another dimension, and could not stay among people

I was calm, certain and strong and managed my intuitions, of choice, thought and imagination. This triangle was my escape from the limited world of earth and made me go to where I saw peace and might understand Theo's enigma.

I did not socialize much. After returning to Los Angeles, I became quiet among my friends. I had little in common with them, talking mainly of purity and love. So I returned to where Gilda had lived. I followed her steps and volunteered to rebuild the small villages devastated by the tsunami.

Previously, I had not been content, but with Theo and I controlling my imagination, thoughts and choices. My joy was profound.

I went to Indonesia to continue Gilda's mission. Being involved made me closer to her. After her death I was different. People told me they couldn't believe I was the William they'd once known.

I transferred my personal assets to Gilda's organization, giving it to them to use in their mission. I didn't care about my business assets back in California. I needed Gilda. I searched for enlightenment and allowed Theo, to align and give meaning to my life.

I gained great satisfaction seeing the beaming smiles on the villagers' faces. Their gratitude let me feel a connection. Caring for a disabled child and helping him stand, I shared his joy in my every pore. When I helped a family send their children to school, the parents' gratitude was so powerful I encouraged others. All my life, living in the confining space of mind and imagination, I had never discovered this joy. The joy of giving is not limited to money, but generosity builds encouragement. Assisting people complements giving, so they recognize their worth and are encouraged to believe in it.

Looking back, I understood how in past years, I'd been afraid to love, fearing those I adored dying and leaving me alone. I was not afraid to love Gilda, even though she was dead, my devotion grew stronger and I felt she watched over me. She granted meaning and light in my life. I was certain she was waiting for my return. My life on earth was just temporary, pulling me closer to discovering Gilda's love. My earthly mission was to put aside fear of love.

I discovered the divinity of my best friend Theo. Theo was I. Knowing he was protecting me, I did not know fear. Discovering this knowledge of my inner strength, my life became magical. When I closed my eyes and my senses, I discovered Theo within. He made me aware of my potential and its supernatural abilities. With this knowledge, I saw Theo's within people around me, hiding and yearning to be discovered.

My imagination turned my every thought into reality. Through my choice and will, I made thoughts materialize. This had not happened before discovering my interior motivation in the form of my old pal and closest friend, my soul Theo.

Each day, morning and night, I walked the beautiful coastline of Indonesia, and sat down in solitude. I watched the sky's vast expanse and it mirrored inside me. I was expansive and aligned with the world around me. Every particle of my surroundings became part of my existence and directly related to me. Upon closing my eyes and meditating, I saw one reality, one universal pattern of energy and creation. I saw beyond physical creation and understood why every human has differing looks, personalities and hopes. I'd already noticed the magnetic power of the solar system and of earth's environment, aligning around each birth. Thinking about this, I understood how two babies born side by side at the same time, would still be different as each received different radiation and influences from surrounding magnetic fields, thus creating different characteristics. Even the wind, position of clouds and the movement of a single leaf on a tree can make a difference in creation. Think of the distance and position of stars and planets subject to that effect. I watched the deep dark sky, sitting by the ocean, staring into its darkest depths, and finding even the darkness has energy I had not previously noticed.

I was fascinated to think the same sky and its shining stars had existed for thousands of years. Someone long ago watched it exactly as I did.

The world stays the same. The sun always rises and sets. We are the ones who change, we who exist within this beautiful harmony and think we own the world. It's a scene change at a theatre where the players and actors change, but the stage remains the same.

I closed my eyes, asking Theo to connect every cell in my body so with his help, I traveled to many places. I merely closed my eyes, searching for Theo within me. He took me into a magnificent world by shutting down my physical senses until I flew with wings. With our combined vitality, we traveled across the universe, watching stars born and stars collapse. We traveled across oceans and breathed the mist of waves. We passed open fields, watching the shining horizon at the edge of the earth. We sat, letting the soft wind lift us toward the clouds, carrying us toward their destiny. We sat on the edge of tall mountains, seeing the world beneath our feet and breathing the crisp air, trying to touch the sky. I loved discovering the strength within me. I connected to passions transforming me into various shapes and figure. I asked myself how, with this abundance of power and motivation, negativity still existed on earth.

I enjoyed my life in Indonesia, experiencing both joy and peace. Now, I didn't need Gilda in my life as she waited on the other side. She was my eternal love and, after I was diagnosed with pneumonia in my final years, I couldn't wait to close my eyes and again feel her love.

—o0o—

Now as Theo, I saw the tunnel, wondering if I was returning. The tunnel's attraction was strong and pulled me in. Looking down, I realized William, in my physical form, had peacefully died in hospital. No one was in the room but I knew he had planned to die peacefully, in Indonesia, of heart failure. It was ironic after losing Gilda, my heart was permanently damaged.

An award for philanthropic efforts remained on William's chest. Gilda's organization and other media chose him as the recipient. A smile lingered on my face as I was happy to go home. William had a smile on his face as he was unafraid to die. He was happy in his last moments, just as I was.

His body was a gift and his ambition and life was immortal. He understood his relationship with me and recognized that he was I.

William was forty-nine years old when diagnosed with valvular heart disease. His body was in agonizing pain but by connecting with me, he was in peace. He shut his thoughts to pain and focused on serenity and aligning with me. Doctors predicted his death years before but were astounded by the way he controlled his thoughts and delayed his death. I'd told William, he would live forever if he focused his mind, but after we traveled to other gateways of life and he'd realized his inner power, he welcomed his physical demise.

On a hot day, he checked into hospital, planning to no longer control his body and give over his body to the earthly disease and die.

After eight months, constantly diagnosed with heart failure, he peacefully passed away, hoping to see Gilda again. A second before his body's last breath, he closed his eyes and said, "Theo, I am you, you are me, now we're going to join together and travel forever." As he closed his eyes, he let go.

—o0o—

Chapter: 22
Theo's return

I knew no one would be at the tunnel to lead me, but I was anxious to see Gilda on the other side. My adoration was so powerful and mesmerizing that I hadn't waited to watch William's burial. I was desperate to feel her course through me. I could only think of her warmth as I'd encountered different energies and experienced minor discomforts in the tunnel.

I expected Keora to meet me, along with my peers and friends. But, I longed to see Gilda. Her spirit was not among my friends and that was strange since in spirit world friends usually participate in the chosen life on earth, especially the role of wife and husband or mother and child, but I had not seen her soul in the spirit world before; I'd never satisfy my thirst for her love and passion.

The magnificence and spectacular radiance of her soul as she left earth haunted my memory. I'd not encountered such intensity except when directly connected to the Source. Even Keora, did not display the same frequency as Gilda. I wondered who she was, as with her love and admiration, her soul should be very advanced. I only cared to see her, feel and adore her.

In the spirit world we do not share the physical connection that earthlings call intimacy, but we experience an intense and incomparable union. Every sense and feeling is vulnerably involved in sharing energy.

Making love on earth, restricted me to my physical senses, yet despite those limitations, it was spiritually amazing as I sought to dissolve into my partner and become one with them. This conjunction is not possible on earth, but in the spirit world, it describes the sensation of loving. Souls merge and coalesce and the sensation is indescribable. I was impatient to enjoy the experience.

As I predicted, Keora met me at the end of the tunnel. I looked around for Gilda but she was not at the gateway although my peers had gathered, welcoming me with their peaceful calm.

I immediately basked in the radiance and the relaxing rays of welcome and once again understood infinity and everlasting truth, where there is no beginning, no end and no limits. All elements connect and link to harmonizing energy without pain and remorse, just advancement. Although I still carried earthly instincts, I was filled with joy and serenity from every corner of the spirit world.

My peers' love filled me, reminding me of the reality of existence and its perpetuity. I had returned to where everything was as I imagined. If I wanted a tree, a tree appeared. If I wished to fly, I flew. Nothing was impossible in our spirit world as everything is formed from our aspirations. If I described the spirit world and expressed it, I'd say, it is what every person wants it to be.

I was thirsty for Gilda and searched for her as I roamed around. I asked Keora if he knew where I might find her. He did not reply but tried calming and relaxing me. He asked others to give me time and space to adjust. I encountered Crystal who'd also been my mother on earth. She was my peer and had been my mate many life cycles ago. Seeing Crystal, sharing my deep gratitude over the passionate lesson of love I'd learned with her, calmed me.

I was delighted to spend time with Crystal, absorbing her affection and quenching my loss of Gilda. She was ecstatic to see me, proudly viewing my advancement and accomplishments.

After spending time with her, I still had to undergo the purification process. A residue of earthly feelings and senses remained as I did not communicate well and my system was slightly off balance.

Feelings of anxiety, homesickness for earth and feeling a loss about Gilda mixed in my soul and I needed to be decontaminated.

On my way to purification, Keora congratulated me. He was proud of what I'd achieved in a single life cycle. Reminding me, "Remember how you resisted returning to earth and choosing a life?"

"Yes, Keora, I wish you'd been on earth with me. At times I was confused and I called for you frequently. I know you heard me and were close, but I wished to actually see you."

"Theo, I was beside you."

"I meant, I wish you'd taken a role in the life I chose. I missed you. I missed everyone here."

"You don't have to admit it, we know, it was not easy. You endured many emotions and we are very proud you completed your mission. I don't need to push you into another mission although I'd have had to if you'd failed."

"Keora, it was difficult fighting emotional battles, especially those involving fear —it's such a strong emotion. Controlling the brain and confronting fear were the most challenging tasks I've ever done, particularly overcoming my fear of love and of losing it. Where is Gilda, Keora? I need her more than my purification."

"Be patient, you'll learn more afterwards and you'll realize how advanced you are. I am extremely proud of you. You have evolved an understanding and are much closer to the Source."

"What do you mean Keora? The most important thing is to grow closer to the Source. I know it is wonderful to gain knowledge of the Source and become enlightened, but how close am I?"

"Remember before you went, the wise leaders offered an incentive to encourage you? They promised a surprise if you accomplished your mission".

"Yes I remember, Keora, what is my surprise?"

He smiled but did not answer.

At the purification door, he told me he'd wait for me. I had anxious expectations about my surprise, but he said I must be patient.

As I took the healing shower, the negative spaces in my soul were recovered and replaced by calmness and serenity. It was strange as I have done this purification process many times in other life cycles, but I never known it like this. As I took the shower, I connected to a core of information. In that shower, I acquired knowledge of the Source greater than ever before. As a thirsty person drinking water, I kept soaking up knowledge and wanted more. The more I gained the more I desired. I became enlightened, the most important state for a soul. In the spirit world, we want to become closer to our creator and share his extraordinary vigor and dynamics. To reach this point, requires greater knowledge of the Source. Souls advance by challenging their energy, gaining supremacy and intensely feeling the Source. On each return from earth, spirits gain strength, acquire knowledge of the spirit world and its creator, understand its mechanism and its evolution. Each advanced soul, becomes enlightened and finally participates in governing the spirit world.

Stepping from the shower to join Keora, I noticed my color was deep purple with arrays of shiny mercury. I was an advanced soul with love bestowed by the Source.

After the purification. I connected to the reality of spirit world. I carried no physical energy and my purification elevated me to an unsullied and pure state of love. Upon meeting my friends, I realized how close we were. My vitality joined us as threads woven into fabric. We channeled into a soft ray of love connecting to the Source. Finally I was back in the realm of love and peace.

Feelings of anxiety, homesickness for earth and a sense of loss over Gilda, mixed in my soul, and I'd needed decontamination.

In that healing shower, I'd replaced my shortcomings and negativity with positive knowledge of the harmonious spirit world and finally understood my task in its creation process.

I was very happy to be back, but the feelings I'd experienced on earth and sensed from Gilda, were not ordinary feelings. I needed to rediscover divine love. I wondered who she was. Maybe she was a motivation granted to me to overcome my fear, but she was too real to be just an inspiration. She had a special glow about her as she'd left her body. Her love was unlike any I had previously encountered. I needed to discover who she was.

Chapter 23: The final episode
Unification

At the gathering, many advanced souls welcomed my return to the spirit world, congratulating me on my success. I was the guest of honor at the award ceremony. I'd been granted knowledge of the spirit world's government while in the healing shower, but I didn't know my role in the creation process. Keora, hovering right by me, was very proud and glowed with joy.

My color was deeper than Keora's, meaning I had advanced beyond him, but in the spirit world no envy or categorization exists. My deep color, indicating my advanced knowledge, didn't mean I was better or due additional respect. All souls share the same respect, because all were created by the Source and carry His energy. In the spirit world no societal levels exist. Spirits are equally respected and loved but share the same desire to know and join the Source. Souls are drops of rain flowing into a stream and finally joining the ocean.

In this final stage of knowledge and advancement, I didn't have to return to earth on further missions. My task was inside the spirit world, unless I volunteered to undertake another life cycle.

The wise spirit who'd encouraged me and helped me pick my challenge, addressed us. He mentioned my reluctance to return to earth, how he'd encouraged my important challenge and how he'd promised a surprise for my successful completion. He enthused over my accomplishment in of overcoming a fear of love.

He said, "Since you were successful, I now reveal my surprise. Theo, we are proud of you, your greater understanding and your newly acquired knowledge of the Source. Since you overcame your challenge and defeated the negative habits of fear, separating it from the divine spirit world, you will now participate in the creation of love."

I was shocked and enthusiastic. I'd now become closer to the Source than I ever thought possible. Creating harmony, love, tenderness, serenity and passion was the Source's primary task and choosing me to assist was the best I might have wished.

He continued, "However Theo, for you to participate love must be involved. The Source is bliss and harmony and to help with your newly assigned task, He created a gift for your accomplishment."

I carefully listened to his every word, impatiently waiting to discover the Source's surprise gift.

Although my thoughts focused on guessing my surprise gift, I slowly grew aware of a familiar wavelength, it was as though I'd touched an electric circuit, and I tried to recognize it. Could it be...? Oh dear, there she was. My long awaited Gilda, was my gift and my promised surprise.

I saw her radiance and once again worshiped every inch of her. Her soul was magnificent and overflowed. Her love was gifted by the Source and put together for me. Not only did she love me, but she was a personalized gift from the Source.

Finally I'm home and never have to return to earth. Although in my last experience on earth as William, I'd experienced true beauty and harmony between a human and its soul. The earth and its beauty combined to recognize higher grades of existence. I am now at ease. I pray for the earth and humans to reach the level of harmony I knew before William's death. I wish all humans could see their spirits and inner souls instead of just flawed physical bodies. I wish they'd realize devotion as part of everyday life. I pray they discover the beauty and splendor each breath gives them with new chances for life. I also hope they appreciate each of the five physical senses and grow their intuitions.

A human is born with a soul, but intuition is a sixth sense. It is well connected in a child, but as the child grows, the soul is distracted by negative thoughts and, is also influenced by parents. Intuition, although controlling the five physical senses, hides beneath those senses and loses its ability and connection. I wish all earthly souls would resist losing the primal sense, enabling humanity's potential and helping see the world in higher dimensions.

Since humanity has been given so many blessings, like its ability to choose, its control of thought, its ability for self-control and its desire to seek a higher power, it has potential to create a world as honest as the spirit world. By controlling its thought and its senses, humanity might even participate in the creation process as it is well within the soul's power. If humans surrendered to their soul's inner bliss, their negative senses and bad habits would be replaced by a powerful blessing advancing the universe. Hatred, fear, judgment and jealousy will be replaced by kindness, bravery, friendship and encouragement.

Until earth combines with the spirit world and realizes its extraordinary potential for advancement and its important role in the creation process, we pray and remain hopeful.

Until we meet again in your real self, I bid you farewell.